THE DANGEROUS VOYAGE

Dave Gustaveson

YWAM Publishing
A Ministry of Youth With A Mission
P.O. Box 55787, Seattle, WA 98155
(206) 771-1153

YWAM Publishing is the publishing ministry of Youth With A Mission. Youth With A Mission (YWAM) is an international missionary organization of Christians from many denominations dedicated to presenting Jesus Christ to this generation. To this end, YWAM has focused its efforts in three main areas: 1) Training and equipping believers for their part in fulfilling the Great Commission (Matthew 28:19). 2) Personal evangelism. 3) Mercy ministry (medical and relief work).

For a free catalog of books and materials write or call:
YWAM Publishing
P.O. Box 55787, Seattle, WA 98155
(206)771-1153 or (800) 922-2143

The Dangerous Voyage

Published by Youth With A Mission Publishing
P.O. Box 55787
Seattle, WA 98155

ISBN 0-927545-82-9

Printed in the United States of America.

To
Don and Deyon
Stevens
of YWAM Mercy Ships
and to all
those who sacrifice their lives
to make voyages of mercy
possible

Other

REEL KIDS
Adventures

The Missing Video ❖ *Cuba*
Mystery at Smokey Mountain ❖ *Philippines*
The Stolen Necklace ❖ *Kenya*
The Mysterious Case ❖ *Colombia*
The Amazon Stranger ❖ *Brazil*
The Dangerous Voyage ❖ *Haiti*
The Lost Diary ❖ *Turkey*
The Forbidden Road ❖ *China*
The Danger Zone ❖ *Vietnam*

Available at your local Christian bookstore or
YWAM Publishing
1(800) 922-2143

Acknowledgments

I love to be close to people who dream big dreams and see visions for reaching the world for Christ. As God gifts us with wonderful and creative imaginations, He desires for them to soar to the highest level of possibility.

Imagine a large ocean liner for Christ. Or what about a whole fleet of ships. Maybe an airline. Can you imagine what the Apostle Paul would do with modern day technology?

I challenge anyone reading this book to launch out to where others haven't. John Kennedy was famous for the words. "Some people see things as they are and ask why. I dream of things that never were and ask why not."

I'm indebted to men like George Verver, Loren Cunningham, Don Stephens, and others. Today, ships of kindness and teams of love sail around the world because men dared to dream. I hope this book ignites that kind of vision in you.

Special thanks to those at Mercy Ships for amazing and valuable insights into the world of sailing. Thanks to Phil Herzog for the sparks that flamed up my imagination. Thanks to David O'Connor for his tireless help and contributions.

Thanks to ship staff and crew like Dan Conners,

Marge Hilton, Becky Bynum, Jon Copley. Also, thanks to Brian Shipley for his insights on Haiti.

Again, thanks to the hard work of those at YWAM Publishing. And again and again, thanks to Shirley Walston for an excellent job of editing. Thanks to Frank Ordaz for his amazing cover designs. Thanks to Vernor Pfau and John Davidson, two prayer warriors who always dare to see the impossible.

Thanks again to my wonderful family who believe with me that kids need to be challenged.

And special thanks to the greatest Captain of them all...the Lord Jesus Christ.

Table of Contents

1. Trapped 9
2. The Takeover .... .21
3. Fire .... .31
4. The Dream .... .39
5. Haiti .... .49
6. Anchored .... .57
7. Boat People .... .63
8. Port–au–Prince .... .73
9. Voodoo .... .83
10. Wounded .... .89
11. Accused .... .95
12. Inspection .... .107
13. Mercy in Action .... .113
14. Betrayal .... .119
15. Darkness .... .127
16. Revolution for Life .... .135

Chapter 1

Trapped

"We're stuck."

Jeff Caldwell mumbled to himself while shuffling along the ship's promenade deck. He stopped to lean over the wooden railing. Squinting his blue eyes, he could see Panama's thick jungle in the distance. He ran his fingers through his short, blond curls in frustration.

The 15-year-old tried to put recent events into perspective. On this hot and humid Tuesday afternoon, July 11, the ship was trapped dead center in the locks of the Panama Canal. This was Jeff's first time on a ship, and he was just beginning to recover from the seasickness that had plagued him since they left Los Angeles.

He yanked at the neck of his t-shirt to let in some air. With his sleeve, he mopped sweat from his brow. The tropical temperature was rising. He knelt on the deck to untie the laces of his Reebok tennis shoes.

Walking along the deck, he found a shady spot and watched the other huge ships anchored in Miraflores Lake. This was supposed to be a staging area for loading and offloading cargo, but it felt like a prison.

From around a corner, his 13-year-old sister, Mindy, appeared and rushed toward him. Dressed in white shorts and a pink blouse, she seemed excited or angry. She was only 5'2", seven inches shorter than her brother. An older gentleman strutted along behind her.

Her braces flashed in the bright tropical sunlight. Her big brown eyes were hidden by the glare reflecting off her glasses, but Jeff could tell something was up. As usual, she yanked nervously at her pale yellow ponytail.

"Feeling better?" Mindy asked. Without waiting for an answer, she absentmindedly patted Jeff on the arm, then turned to the stranger. "This is Harold Simpson. He's a volunteer doctor on the ship. He just met our beloved K.J., and now he wants to talk to you."

Jeff nodded, wondering what his best friend had done now. "Nice to meet you, sir."

Dr. Simpson was slightly shorter than Jeff and looked like he was in his mid-thirties. He was dressed in black slacks and a white shirt. He stood with his shoulders back and his chest stuck out. Jeff was reminded of those birds who plumps up his feathers to make himself look bigger. But it was Dr. Simpson's cold, green eyes that sent a chill down the nape of Jeff's neck. They seemed to stare right through Jeff.

"You're the leader of some kind of media club?" Dr. Simpson scoffed. "But you're just a kid! Are there no adults with you?"

"Our team leader couldn't make the voyage," Jeff replied calmly. "But he's meeting us in Haiti. Is there a problem?"

"Yes. There's a problem! That dingy dark-haired brat—your cameraman, he calls himself—just pointed his camera in my face! Without asking permission! What do you plan to do with the photos?" Dr. Simpson's long oval face and the way he pursed his lips made him look menacing.

Jeff shifted anxiously on his long legs. He wanted some clue from Mindy about what was going on, but this wasn't the time. Instead, he took a deep breath and looked Dr. Simpson in the eye.

"We're called the Reel Kids," Jeff began, "from Los Angeles. We film videos in difficult situations around the world. They are shown to inspire others to help in the work."

The disgust evident on Dr. Simpson's face made Jeff feel defensive. But he remembered that being stuck in the locks was making everyone tense, so he just smiled.

"Well," Dr. Simpson huffed, "I'm going to the captain about this! A bunch of kids have no business on a ship by themselves. And you have no right to photograph people who don't wish to be photographed!"

He turned on his heel and stomped off.

Mindy flung her hands in the air and whispered, "That K.J. has done it again! He gets us in trouble every time."

She took off after Dr. Simpson, trying to calm him down. Jeff shook his head and returned to the railing.

"Oh brother," he muttered under his breath. "It's going to be one of those trips again."

As he thought about it, though, a smile broke across his face. He realized how lucky they were to be part of the club...and on a ship, even if they were stuck.

Jeff thought about his first photography class years ago. Warren Russell had been his teacher, and since then Warren had radically changed Jeff's life.

Warren launched the Reel Kids Club with the idea of taking high schoolers on international adventures. On assignment, they employed their communication skills to produce videos of their journeys. They shared their faith in God at the same time.

Jeff knew part of the reason he loved the club was his natural interest in media. Both Jeff and Mindy were influenced by their parents' careers in media. Their dad was an anchorman on a local television station, and their mom worked as a part-time news correspondent. Both parents were thrilled with the opportunities the Reel Kids Club presented.

The club met off campus, but had permission to borrow the school's media equipment. The principal liked the idea of offering kids practical experience.

The club usually traveled during school breaks. But this trip was very different. Totally unplanned.

Hurricane Audrey had violently struck Haiti, killing hundreds and wiping out thousands of homes. The next day, Warren had received a call from the director of the 12,086 ton M.V. *Charity II.*

The *Charity II* was a mercy ship. It delivered food and building supplies, brought volunteers to help, and provided medical assistance to developing nations all over the world. Powered by two Fiat diesel engines, the 1955 vessel could carry three cargo holds full of supplies. The ship was part of a large mission organization called Mission International—or M.I. for short. With over 8000 volunteers worldwide, they worked in every kind of mission and relief work.

During the voyage from L.A., the staff had told dozens of miraculous stories of things God had done on their journeys. After hearing their stories, Jeff thought about serving with M.I. himself. Some staff were short-term, while others served for a couple of years or longer. Everyone aboard volunteered their time, raising their own financial support.

The organization had scores of bases worldwide and operated three other ships. *Charity II* was chosen for this trip because it was closest to Haiti when the hurricane hit. The boat was also equipped with a 40-bed hospital ward to handle surgeries and medical emergencies.

Warren had been asked to assemble a film crew to record the ship's efforts in Haiti. The call came so suddenly that Warren's schedule wouldn't allow him to sail with the club. But he was scheduled to arrive by plane in Haiti a few hours earlier than the ship. Dan Johnson, the ship's director, had volunteered to keep an eye on the team.

Just days before leaving for Haiti, Jeff, Mindy and K.J. had returned from a trip to Mexico. They had planned to mow lawns, ride mountain bikes, and go to the beach for the remainder of July. But they knew they couldn't pass this opportunity up.

Mindy strolled up to the railing beside Jeff and sighed. "Not only do we have a problem with Dr. Simpson, but the political situation is getting worse by the minute."

"Yeah? Anything new?"

"Political situations around here are very unstable. I just heard that the Panamanian authorities could keep us in the locks for weeks."

Jeff knew his sister was frightened. He needed to collect his thoughts, but his frustration grew by the moment. During the night, the ship had sailed through the east locks of the Panama Canal. But now they were stuck in Miraflores Lake.

"Mindy, explain the locks to me, will ya?" Jeff finally said. "If L.A. is west, how did we enter the locks from the east?"

"I did a report on this once," Mindy replied, perking up at the chance to share her research. "The canal is a set of three lock systems. You know, where the water is closed off and let up and down?"

Jeff nodded.

"Okay," Mindy continued. "The country of Panama kind of twists upward to the right." She used her hands and body to show him what she meant. "Ships have to travel around the land, which dips south. They end up on the east, then the canal takes them west, sort of northwest."

"Got it," Jeff answered. "Now tell me why they've stopped us."

"I don't think it's normal to have been stopped without warning. It's supposed to take about fifteen hours to get through the locks—about half of it waiting. I hear there's political unrest and military fighting on the eastern end of the Canal right now."

Jeff glanced at his watch. "It's almost two. Fourteen hundred hours by ship time. We've been in this one spot for six long hours!"

Mindy nodded.

"How could this happen?" Jeff burst out. "Maybe Dr. Simpson is right. Maybe we should've stayed home and been content with our Mexico trip this summer."

"Hey," Mindy patted his arm. "We've been on tough trips before." Her brow creased. "But I'm getting worried. Mom and dad won't be happy when they hear what's going on."

Jeff scratched his head. "I admire them for standing behind us on these trips, even when we get in a jam. But this could be our worst situation yet."

"Yeah. Warren will probably now get to Haiti *way* before us."

"You're right," Jeff agreed, staring into space. "M.I.'s Haiti staff is supposed to pick him up, but he can't do much without the ship."

"Think the voodoo in Haiti has something to do with all this?" Mindy mused. "Michelle might be able to tell us more about it. Wish I'd had time to research properly."

Jeff looked up to see K.J. and Michelle coming toward them. Michelle was a 17-year-old Haitian who'd been on the ship's staff for nearly a year. For this trip, she'd become a part of their team.

"Hey," Jeff nodded in the direction of his best friend. "Here comes our ditsy cameraman now."

K.J.'s real name was Kyle James Baxter. He was wearing jeans shorts and a t-shirt with a picture of a truck with huge tires. Written across the front was the question, "Driven over a Ford lately?" But no matter how he dressed, what everyone noticed about K.J. was his infectious smile and the way he bounced in his tennis shoes. Attached to K.J.'s hand, as usual, was his Canon 8 camcorder. He was the team's cameraman, and though he was only 14, he had developed a unique talent for film.

K.J. also had a real knack for getting into trouble, but he was so charming no one could stay mad at him for long. And to his credit, he would film anything in sight, no matter how dangerous.

Jeff smiled at Michelle, knowing how important she was to the trip. Because she'd grown up in Haiti, she spoke the language and knew how to get around like no one else did. She was 5'4", slightly shorter than K.J. Her round face was the color of roasted coffee beans, and her smile showcased perfect teeth. She dressed in radiant, bright colors, and her black curly hair was pulled neatly away from her face.

When she was 12, Michelle's parents had fled Haiti to escape the cruel reign of a former leader. The family had become American citizens. Because Mission International had once helped them, her parents worked as volunteers in the ship's home office. After her early graduation from high school, Michelle had joined the crew on *Charity II*.

Dan Johnson and Warren had invited Michelle to join the Reel Kids Club for this trip. She was excellent with the camcorder, so she and K.J. were gathering twice the footage.

Jeff noticed the pale look on K.J.'s face. "How you feeling, K.J.?"

"Still yucky, thanks," K.J. groaned. "I don't think I'm made for sailing. There's nothing left in my stomach."

"Why don't you get something to eat?" Mindy teased.

"Yeah, right." K.J. rolled his eyes in disgust. "So you can watch me throw up again? I don't have an iron stomach like you."

Jeff chuckled. "We've raced for the railing too many times, haven't we, buddy? But I feel better since I ate some crackers. You should try some."

K.J. growled a little. "No thanks. Sleeping away this morning was what the doctor ordered."

Michelle giggled.

"Speaking of the doctor," Mindy smiled wistfully, "Michelle, do you know anything about a Dr. Simpson? He almost took Jeff's head off. He's mad because K.J. got him on film."

"That old grouch," K.J. said. "He was only playing shuffleboard on the deck. I don't have any idea why he was so mad. Maybe he's on the FBI's Most Wanted list or something."

Michelle pursed her lips while rubbing her chin. "I've never seen him before this trip," she said in her charming French accent. "He's one of twenty volunteer doctors along on this trip. We always have volunteers when there's something like a hurricane. Especially medical personnel. He came aboard in L.A. when you did. We don't really know them like we know our staff."

"He thinks we ought to be with an adult," Jeff put in. "But he did seem to be overreacting, all right. There's something weird about him. Be careful around him, huh, K.J.?"

Michelle raised her eyebrows slightly. "Once in a while we get a strange one."

"He seemed like a hurt person to me," Mindy put in. "Like he's carrying a huge chip on his shoulder."

"Well," Michelle said. "We'll keep an eye on him so he won't cause a mutiny."

Everyone laughed—except Jeff. Looking up to the bridge, he saw a huge, blue smokestack pointing toward the heavens. Painted on it was M.I.'s logo—the black outline of a globe with a flaming torch covering it.

Jeff glanced at the portholes lining the sides of the massive white vessel. The words *Charity II* were inscribed in bold letters on the hull. "This ship is amazing."

"It's a gift." Michelle smiled. "Hundreds, maybe thousands, of donations from caring people made it possible."

"What I want to know," K.J. said with a grin, "is how much it costs to fill the gas tank."

"About one hundred thousand dollars," Michelle whispered, leaning towards him.

Everyone gasped in unison.

Jeff stared blankly. "You're kidding, right?"

Michelle laughed, shaking her head. "When we say 'fill her up,' it means big bucks."

"How much cargo does she hold?" Mindy wanted to know.

"About 1800 tons."

Jeff was in awe. Though the ship was only a big hunk of metal, he knew the work it did was vital to God.

Using his telephoto lens, K.J. started videotaping the other ships anchored out in the lake. Mindy and Jeff listened carefully while Michelle offered more details about the *Charity II*.

With a huge smile on her face, she described feeding programs and the distribution of clothing and supplies. She told of operations done nearly every day in the ship's hospital.

Jeff waited for her to pause before he asked, "I heard Haiti gave itself to Satan years ago. Is that true?"

"Yes," Michelle answered faintly. "History says that a man named Boukman made a sacrifice to Satan two hundred years ago. Haitians felt it was the only way they could gain freedom from their cruel French slave masters."

"Did the sacrifice work?" Mindy asked.

"They think it did," Michelle said softly. "In thirteen years, the Haitians had defeated the French with a cruel vengeance. All this happened under Napoleon's rule. People say this defeat changed the course of American history."

"American history?" Jeff frowned.

"Because the battle in Haiti cost the French so

much, Napoleon decided to sell Louisiana to America. It's called the Louisiana Purchase."

"I didn't know that," K.J. remarked, pulling his camera away from his face.

"Haiti became the first black republic," Michelle said. "But it has been a nightmare of voodoo, black magic, and demonic forces ever since."

"What do you mean?" Mindy looked concerned.

"You wouldn't know it at first. Most people are either Catholic or Protestant. But everybody believes in voodoo too."

Suddenly, Dr. Simpson hurried up to the group. "Do you kids know what's going on?" he huffed.

Jeff shrugged his shoulders, while everyone stared.

Dr. Simpson looked disgusted. "Dan Johnson just called an emergency meeting."

"Really?" Jeff said in surprise. "When?"

Dr. Simpson shook his head. "In ten minutes. And it sounds like bad news."

Chapter 2

The Takeover

"What do you mean?" Mindy demanded to know.

"Find out for yourself," Dr. Simpson called over his shoulder as he strutted off.

Sitting in the international lounge on the promenade deck, Jeff looked around the meeting room while others were filing in. The walls and ceiling were painted marine white. Along one wall, a large photo of the *Charity II* was surrounded by photos of

21

the other ships in Mission International's fleet. An eight-foot, red-and-blue banner hung behind the podium. First Corinthians 13 was neatly embroidered across it.

As he read the scripture verses, Jeff realized why the ship was named *Charity*. Charity meant love in action.

Jeff saw Captain Davidson and Dan Johnson chatting in the front. As the ship's director, Dan was in charge of all the ship's operations except the actual sailing. He had wavy blond hair, a well-trimmed reddish beard, and blue eyes that seemed to smile when he was talking. His six-foot muscular frame commanded the attention of his staff. For eight years, he had lovingly served on the ship.

Jeff thought Captain Davidson was in great shape for a man in his late fifties. The captain was solidly built, but he looked small beside Dan. Twenty-five years at sea had etched rugged lines in his tan face. His graying hair and mustache and large, dark eyes gave him dignity.

Finally, everyone was seated. The room quieted when Captain Davidson made his way to the podium. He grinned as he glanced over some papers. "There's been no change in our situation, but I can give you a few details. We've been in radio contact with two other ships. They're worried that this problem could last for days."

A murmur went through the crowd.

Clearing his throat, Captain Davidson went on. "We're doing the best we can. Since Miraflores Lake is fresh water, we'll use this time—and our biggest hoses—to wash down the entire ship. I'll assign crew members to start that process."

Jeff leaned closer to K.J. "That sounds like fun. Maybe we can help."

"I'll do the filming," K.J. whispered.

After Captain Davidson finished, Dan came forward. "We need prayer support. We know these problems are a direct attack on our mission to Haiti. We feel it's related to Satan's voodoo influence."

Jeff felt the prickle of goose bumps on his forearms.

Dan looked boldly at the crowd. "We must win this battle in prayer. We're calling a special meeting at sixteen-hundred hours. With the exception of Captain Davidson and his men, we'd like you all to join us."

Jeff turned around to look at Dr. Simpson. He was surprised to lock eyes with him. The doctor just glared.

"We've got one more thing to pray about," Dan continued, pulling Jeff's attention once more to the front of the room. "Another powerful hurricane is forming in the Caribbean. Even if the canal opens, we may have to face the storm."

Loud whispering instantly filled the room.

Dan waited for silence before continuing. "This isn't the first time we've faced obstacles like this. God will see us through this crisis. Please break up into small groups and pray."

Chatter filled the room as everyone regrouped.

While Jeff was scooting a chair around, he caught a glimpse of Dr. Simpson rushing to the front. From what Jeff could tell, the doctor was protesting Dan's request to pray. And he seemed really angry.

As he continued to watch the interaction between the two men, Jeff was amazed. With a kind expression on his face, Dan listened carefully and nodded. Finally, Dr. Simpson threw up his hands and bustled away.

"Maybe we should talk to that guy," Jeff whispered to Michelle. She nodded.

Dan and Captain Davidson came over, and Dan smiled at everyone. "I'm sorry. I probably wouldn't have asked you to go if I'd known all this was going to happen."

Jeff put his hands up, grinning. "We've been on tough trips." Then he laughed. "Well, never on a ship. But we're glad to be here. We want to help any way we can."

K.J. turned to Dan with an excited look. "Can we film the crew hosing down the ship?"

Both Dan and the captain laughed out loud.

"Sure," Dan said. "Let us know if you need anything. We want to make the best of this for you."

The captain motioned to K.J. and Michelle. They tiptoed out to join the ship's crew.

"Now. Let's get busy talking to the Lord," Dan said, grabbing a chair to join what was left of the circle.

"That's one of our favorite things to do," Jeff said. "And we want to win this battle. The people of Haiti need us."

Dan nodded as he bowed his head. The one hundred-member staff was already praying. Jeff sat on the edge of his seat. Mindy was right next to him.

"Lord," a woman from the kitchen staff prayed, "You're greater than the darkness trying to stop us."

Jeff whispered, "Amen." Around the crowded room, people were praying and cheering. Soon, Jeff couldn't hold back any longer. He had to pray. Lifting his head, he began, "Lord, we pray against the voodoo powers in Haiti. We know Your name is greater. Show the people of Haiti who really reigns on earth."

After finishing his prayer, he looked at Mindy. She looked frightened.

"Are you okay, sis?" he asked.

"What Michelle told us about Haiti dedicating their island to Satan frightens me," she whispered. "I'm not sure I want to go. Maybe God is trying to stop us."

Jeff's eyes softened with compassion. "Hey. That rattled me too. But I know Jesus will protect us."

"I hope so," Mindy sighed. "I hope so."

As the prayer time continued, Jeff wondered about K.J. and Michelle. Finally, he decided to check on them. He raced down the long hallway toward the sound of gushing water. Turning a corner, he ran straight into K.J.

"Are you guys done shooting?" Jeff asked.

K.J. nodded. "We got some great shots. Michelle is finishing up on the starboard side. I was just heading back to the prayer meeting."

"Let's go," Jeff urged. "It's been really good."

As Jeff and K.J. headed for the stairs, they heard loud voices coming from an open cabin. Creeping closer, Jeff could tell it was Dr. Simpson. The door was open at least a foot. With K.J. right behind him, Jeff leaned in to catch what was being said. He motioned for K.J. to have a look, and they both stared into the room.

Dr. Simpson sat with six other volunteers in the

crowded cabin. Instinctively, K.J. raised the camera to his face.

"These guys have no idea what they're doing," Dr. Simpson was saying. "They're going to get us all killed. We could be imprisoned. And you've heard how they treat Americans in foreign prisons."

Jeff froze, not knowing what to do. Just then, Mindy appeared and ran over to join them. Jeff put his index finger to his mouth to keep her quiet.

"What are you guys doing?" she whispered.

"Dr. Simpson is stirring up others against Dan and Captain Davidson."

Jeff looked back toward K.J. He couldn't believe his eyes. A cold chill swept over him.

Dr. Simpson stood there, with a firm grip on K.J.'s camera. The others peered out the door.

"What do you brats think you're doing?" Dr. Simpson demanded.

Jeff's pulse quickened, and his face turned red. K.J. tried to wrestle his camera away, but Dr. Simpson was too strong. With her eyes as big as the frames on her glasses, Mindy stood as still as a statue.

Jeff's mind raced wildly. Then he stood tall. "We heard you, Dr. Simpson. You're causing trouble here. Starting a rebellion. Or should I call it a mutiny?"

K.J. finally jerked the camera away. Angrily, Dr. Simpson turned to Jeff with a mocking laugh. "These leaders don't know what they're doing. I can't believe they called a prayer meeting! They should be calling for the U.S. Army, not God."

"Dr. Simpson." Jeff was shocked. "Didn't you know this ship is part of a Christian organization?"

Dr. Simpson shook his head. "All Americans are

Christians, aren't they? Your so-called leaders need some common sense. I wish I could get a plane out of here."

An idea hit Jeff. "Why don't we talk to Dan Johnson? He can probably arrange to get you off the ship."

"Look!" Dr. Simpson became livid. "I don't need help from a bunch of kids! You're not to mention this to anyone, or you'll have me to contend with. And I want that videotape. Now."

K.J. quickly stepped back.

"Look. Dr. Simpson," Jeff blurted. "What you do is your business. I hope you can find a way out of here. But you must realize, this ship is too small for you to cause trouble."

Dr. Simpson chuckled. Then his smile turned into a glare, and his voice dropped in pitch. "Give me the tape."

K.J.'s eyes danced.

Jeff was frozen for a second. "Why do you want the tape?" he finally asked. "We're filming lots of things. Besides, the captain knew we filmed the washing of the ship. He'll wonder if it's not on the video."

Dr. Simpson's left eye began to twitch. "All right. We'll all stand here and watch you erase what you just saw here. You have no business filming me. I could sue you."

Jeff glanced at K.J., who looked like he couldn't make up his mind whether or not to do what the doctor said.

"Go ahead and erase it," Jeff said. "We know what he said anyway."

Jeff could almost see steam coming from Dr. Simpson's ears. Everyone watched K.J. push buttons and rewind the tape. In the back of Jeff's mind, he wondered if K.J. had really erased what he'd filmed or just made it look like he had.

"Good," Dr. Simpson said simply. "Now get out of here."

Jeff, K.J., and Mindy rushed off. As they rejoined the prayer meeting, Jeff couldn't help but wonder why Dr. Simpson didn't want to be filmed.

❖❖❖❖❖❖❖

By nine o'clock that night, Jeff was beginning to think Tuesday would never end. The ship's decks were thoroughly cleaned, and a late buffet dinner was served. After everyone had eaten, Michelle offered to complete the club's tour of the ship.

The reflected moonlight in the ship's pool nearly drew the four of them in for a swim, but they decided to wait for sunshine. They toured empty classrooms and an enormous kitchen bustling with people washing dishes and mopping floors. Neither K.J.'s camera nor Mindy's notepad missed a detail.

"Do you think we could see the hospital ward?" Mindy asked, tapping her chin with a pencil. "Before I discovered computers, I'd thought about becoming a nurse."

Michelle smiled and nodded. The team followed her down the steps to B-deck. She led the way through the big, white door of the hospital. Jeff studied the room full of beds and medical supplies.

"Looks like any other hospital," Mindy observed.

"Smells like one too—all clean and antiseptic. It's just a little smaller."

"What kind of operations do they do?" K.J. asked.

Michelle walked to a counter and flipped open a picture book. "Mostly reconstructive surgeries," She said softly. "Eye surgeries and cleft lip and palates. This book is filled with photos of patients before and after their operations."

As she turned the pages, everyone gasped.

"This little girl had a tumor. This is her before."

Jeff stood there with his mouth open. A growth as big as a grapefruit bulged out of the side of her face.

When Michelle turned the page, Mindy jumped with excitement. "Look, it's gone! Completely gone."

A tear slid down Michelle's round face. "I'm sorry. We do lots of operations like this," she said wiping her eyes. "Seeing the kids' faces always touches my heart. They get a new start on life."

Suddenly, an announcement came over the loud speaker. Another meeting was being called for ten o'clock. Jeff looked at his watch. It was 9:45.

❖❖❖❖❖❖❖

Sitting down, Jeff forced his tired eyes to sweep around the room. He spotted Dr. Simpson sitting with the same group of volunteers who had been in the room with him earlier. Dr. Simpson sneered at him, and Jeff quickly turned around.

Dan approached the podium to address the

curious crowd. "Please forgive the lateness of the meeting, but we've just received news I knew you'd want to hear. Good news and some sad news too."

Everyone leaned forward. Jeff felt electricity in the air.

"Panama's political crisis has been resolved, at least for now." Dan smiled. "Canal authorities have given us permission to continue through the locks in a few hours."

Everyone applauded. K.J. high-fived Jeff and Mindy. Michelle giggled. Some of the staff members hugged each other.

But Jeff knew Dan wasn't finished.

"Captain Davidson will fill you in a few details in a minute. But I have to tell you one more thing," Dan continued.

Everyone waited, holding their breath. Dan's smile had disappeared. His eyes were sad. Silence fell over the crowd. "Four hours ago, a major problem arose in Haiti."

The room was totally quiet.

"There's been a coup."

Chapter 3

Fire

K.J. jerked sharply on Jeff's arm. "Wait a minute. What does he mean?"

With chills, Jeff looked at his friend. "The military has taken over Haiti."

"We don't care who's runnin' the place, do we? Will it affect us?"

"I don't know," Jeff said, trying to shush him. "I'm sure Dan will tell us."

The room was filled with commotion.

Dan waited for quiet, then pulled the microphone close. "The hurricane gave the army a chance to turn against the government. Now there's a new leader in Haiti."

A crew member raised his hand. "Are we still going?"

Jeff's heartbeat quickened. Though frightened, he didn't want to cancel the whole trip.

Dan put his hands up to quiet the crowd before he spoke. "We're not changing our plans. The people need us more than ever. We believe the new leader will welcome us since we're a mercy ship. If they don't, we can always go to the Dominican Republic. It's just east of Haiti, but on the same island."

Again, noise filled the room.

Suddenly, a terrifying thought struck Jeff. He stared at his watch. "Oh no," he cried, turning to K.J. and Mindy. "Warren landed in Haiti before the coup took place."

Quickly, Jeff raised his hand. After Dan acknowledged him, he stood shakily to his feet. "Do you know the exact time the coup took place?"

"All we heard was four hours ago, but that was just before we called the meeting. We hear the fighting is still going on."

Jeff grabbed the chair in front of him for support. "Then I have a prayer request. Our leader, Warren, wasn't able to sail with us. He flew out of L.A. this morning. His plane was scheduled to arrive in Haiti at six o'clock this evening. He's probably in danger."

"Not good news. We'll pray for his protection," Dan said.

Dr. Simpson stood up and waited for the crowd to quiet down. Then he started lecturing. "I have something to say about all of this. First, I don't think these kids, this so-called team, should even be here. It's too dangerous."

The air became thick with tension.

"And I think it's foolish to go on to Haiti," Dr. Simpson went on. "We need to turn around and head straight back to the U.S. while we have a chance."

Everyone looked stunned. No one said a word.

"It's crazy to think we'll be safe!" Dr. Simpson's voice got louder. "And don't forget about that other hurricane on the way."

With a tight jaw, Jeff looked straight ahead. He knew Dr. Simpson was making sense, even though he was out of control. He hoped Dan would know what to do.

Dan listened politely and smiled a calming smile. "First of all, the Reel Kids Club are our special guests. We'll make sure they're not in any danger. Secondly, we are monitoring the situation in Haiti. We're all committed to being in the center of God's will. We won't go ahead unless it's safe."

Shaking his head in disgust, Dr. Simpson plunked down in his chair.

"We're preparing to sail," Dan went on. "If any of you volunteers want to leave, I'll personally make those arrangements in the Dominican Republic. If there are any urgent changes, we'll announce them. Meanwhile, pray for Warren and our permanent team in Haiti. Then get some sleep."

Jeff was proud of Dan. He was a secure leader who was not afraid to make decisions. As the meeting broke up, Jeff looked over at Michelle. "You've lived in Haiti half your life, Michelle. What do you think happened?"

"Haiti is famous for kicking out leaders,"

Michelle said. "The former leader was really into voodoo. He was planning another ceremony to dedicate the island to Satan."

"Wow," K.J. cried. "Wasn't once enough?"

"Maybe things will work out for the best," Jeff said. "This coup could be an answer to our prayers."

Michelle rolled her eyes. "I don't know. The military can be pretty cruel. I wish I knew who took over."

"So Warren might be in a lot of trouble," Mindy said quietly.

"What will they do to him? And the team that's already there?" Jeff wanted to know.

"I wish I knew." Michelle shook her head. "We'll just have to wait and see."

"What do we do now?" Mindy asked.

"Pray," Jeff said. "And pray hard."

Just before midnight, the team finished praying.

"Hey, Michelle. Think the captain's given the final word to sail yet?" Jeff asked.

"You'll know when it happens. There are loud speakers everywhere."

"I'm exhausted, but there's no way I could sleep until I know what's going on."

"Hey!" Michelle snapped her fingers. "I haven't shown you the engine room yet. Let's go. We can't go inside, but we can watch from the doorway."

"Great idea," K.J. said, grabbing his camera.

Everyone scrambled out of the room. On the way down the stairs, Jeff heard a loud humming noise.

"We're almost there," Michelle said over her shoulder.

Stopping at a doorway that seemed to pulse with deafening mechanical noises, she pointed inside. "This is one of the two main engines," she yelled to be heard over the racket.

Jeff couldn't believe it. He'd always loved playing with engines, but he'd never seen anything like this. Massive metal parts were fitted together, all moving in unison. The engine was as big as a two-story house.

Everything, including the engineers, was blackened with grease. The smell of diesel fuel was nearly strong enough to knock them over. Huge tools were organized in large closets. Massive bolts and nuts the size of dinner plates lay scattered on a wooden bench.

"How do these guys do this?" Mindy asked loudly, watching men scurry around in greasy jumpsuits.

"Everyone is different," Michelle said. "These guys love it down here. The diesel smells, dirt, and grease. They even love the noise."

Suddenly, the captain's voice boomed out. Everyone stopped to listen. They hurried up the stairs to get away from the noise.

"We've taken everything into consideration." The captain's voice echoed throughout the ship. "We believe we're to sail to Haiti as soon as possible."

A cheer drowned out the engine noise from below.

Jeff's heart almost skipped a beat. He wondered what adventures lie ahead.

The ship's engines roared. K.J. grabbed his camcorder, and they all headed to the main deck. One huge link at a time, the anchors were hoisted up. Both K.J. and Michelle had cameras running. Jeff wondered what Dr. Simpson would do now.

It was 2:30 in the morning, but still the team couldn't sleep. Large beams like streetlights lit up the jungle shores on both sides of the canal. The moon was the color of bright, cold silver. The ship moved at a slow five knots an hour.

"It's amazing." Mindy peered out at the dark jungle. "I can't believe we're here."

She rested her arms on the railing and watched the jungle pass. "Did you know that between 1907 and 1914, while it was being built, they discovered that the mosquito carried malaria? Then they used all kinds of oils and stuff to draw the mosquito into the water to kill it."

A smile broke across Jeff's face. He stood back and looked into his little sister's eyes. "I can't believe all the things you remember."

Mindy laughed. "Thousands of men died of malaria and yellow fever during the building of this canal," she contiued. "They used only donkeys, trains, wagons, and dynamite. Modern equipment hadn't been invented yet."

As Jeff looked ahead, he saw they were entering the last locks.

"So why do they use locks, Mindy?" K.J. asked with his camera in her face.

"The water levels between the Atlantic and Pacific Oceans are different. It requires five locks. Three on the western side and two on the east."

Jeff smiled at his sister. "I don't know about you guys, but I'm tired. I haven't slept for much too long. I'm about to collapse."

Mindy agreed. "Let's get some sleep."

K.J. lowered his camera to his side. "Yeah. I guess I'm ready for that."

❖❖❖❖❖❖❖

As if it were an arrow aimed through the port-hole, sunshine stabbed Jeff in the shoulder. He awakened from a terrifying dream. Shaking himself, he realized the dream wasn't real. He was dripping with perspiration.

Peering over the edge of his top bunk, he saw K.J. still sleeping peacefully. The metal bunks, equipped with netting to hold sailors in bed during high seas, were bolted to the wall.

He looked around the cramped cabin. A tiny sink squatted in a corner. A chair, a shelf that served as a desk, and a couple of hooks on the wall were the only furniture. Beside the door was a closet about the size of his school locker.

Trying to clear his head, Jeff glanced at his watch. It was just past ten, finally Wednesday morning. Peering out the small porthole, he guessed they were headed northeast in the Caribbean Sea—on a straight course for Haiti.

Jeff felt numbed by the dream. He couldn't shake the feeling of terror. He'd seen a long pole with a large snake slithering down it. At the base of the pole, he'd seen Warren trying to run from the snake.

In the dream, Warren had been in trouble. Jeff had seen a small flash of white light, but the snake wasn't even frightened of it. But then, as the light grew bigger, the snake fled.

Jeff was glad the dream had ended well, but it had been a fearful experience. He was totally exhausted. As he lay thinking about it, he heard K.J. moan and roll over.

Jeff couldn't wait any longer, so he leaned over. "Wake up, K.J. Wake up."

Just as K.J. opened one eye, they were startled by the ship's alarm bell. Then a voice came over the loud speaker. Jeff listened carefully. The words were frighteningly clear. "Fire. Fire. Fire," the cry wailed. "The ship's on fire."

Chapter 4

The Dream

"Proceed to your assigned emergency stations."
Jeff's mind swirled in confusion. His heart filled with panic. Suddenly, he heard a loud knock on the cabin door.

Quickly, Jeff jumped from his bunk and grabbed his pants. "Just a minute," he called.

The knock grew louder and faster. "Jeff! K.J.! Hurry!" Michelle cried from the other side of the door.

As Jeff bent over to shove his foot in his pantleg, K.J. jumped out of his bunk, and they both went sprawling to the floor. It took a few seconds to sort themselves out and get into their pants. Jeff grabbed a shirt, any shirt, as he yanked the door open.

K.J. ignored a shirt, but he snatched all the equipment he could carry and handed Jeff a bag on the way out. Jeff knew he'd never leave his camera on a burning ship.

Michelle was shaking. Terror filled her big eyes. "Quick. We've got to get out of here. This is not a drill. There's a fire near the engine room. If they don't put it out, the ship will go down! Fast. Let's go."

In the ship's hallway, people were scrambling. Some ran, while others peered out of their doors.

"Wait! Where's Mindy?" Jeff screamed after a step or two.

"She's coming," Michelle yelled over her shoulder. "I woke her on the way to your cabin. Let's go! My job is to get you out of here."

Racing down the hallway, they skidded to stop at Mindy's door.

Jeff was already out of breath. Beating on the door, Jeff screamed, "Mindy! Are you in there? Hurry!"

With her blonde hair flying, Mindy raced out. She flung her computer bag to Jeff on the way by. Jeff grabbed her arm and started after the others. Stumbling up the stairs behind Michelle, he couldn't dismiss the memory of his dream.

The vision of the snake in his dream began to engulf him. It seemed the snake was chasing them. But he snapped his thoughts off, running for his life.

"We've gone through the fire drill many times," Michelle called over her shoulder when they reached the top deck. "Head over there toward those lifeboats."

They all caught their breath. Jeff saw clouds of thick, black smoke pouring from one of the hatches. People raced from the area like frightened ants.

Jeff noticed an odd assortment of shorts, t-shirts, and dresses, but everyone was dressed.

"After our late night," Jeff said between breaths. "I expected to see everyone in bathrobes."

"We are trained to be ready to leave the ship in any emergency," Michelle said, looking down at her long, pink cotton nightshirt. "This is one of four emergency spots on the ship. Only the captain will give the final word to abandon ship."

"Has there been a fire before?" Mindy cried, pulling her hair out of her face.

"Only once," Michelle said bravely. "But the fire team had it out in twenty minutes. We didn't need the lifeboats."

"Fire team?" K.J. chirped. "Where do they come from?"

"All of our crew is trained for a number of jobs. One of them is fire fighting."

Jeff glanced around. He saw everyone gathering in emergency groups. A few faces were stained with tears. Others prayed fervently. Jeff looked across the deck. A frantic Dr. Simpson paced the deck with his arms across his chest.

In spite of his stance, the doctor's eyes gave him away. They were big, round, and wide open, but he wouldn't look Jeff in the eye. Suddenly an awful thought hit Jeff. Maybe Dr. Simpson had started the fire.

Jeff tried to shake the thought. Looking toward the fire, he thought the clouds of smoke were smaller than they'd been earlier. More men ran toward the fire with additional fire extinguishers.

Dressed in firefighter's coats, hats, and large boots, they worked tirelessly. Everyone watched, hoping for the best. There was dead silence in the crowd. Jeff prayed without moving his lips.

"I hope everybody got out of their cabins," Mindy whispered.

Michelle nodded, finally able to breathe again. "We have an excellent fire team. Every room is checked out. We're each responsible for certain others. I'm sure everyone got out."

Jeff looked at his watch. It was close to eleven. Already, the team had fought the fire for 45 minutes.

The silence grated on his nerves. He wanted to help, to do something. But he was confined to wait with the others. Some staff prayed, some laughed among themselves. Dr. Simpson never stopped pacing.

"Michelle, are we going to be okay?" Mindy finally asked.

"It's looking better," she sighed. "But a ship fire can flame up again in seconds. The captain won't give the word until it's okay. Until then, we must be ready to enter the lifeboats."

Jeff studied the smoke clouds again. They were definitely smaller now.

Finally, the captain's voice crackled over the speaker. "The fire is out," he cried. "God has helped us."

Everyone cheered in unison. People danced with delight.

"Please stay where you are." The captain's voice bellowed over the noise. "We're inspecting the ship for damages. Thanks to our sprinkler system and one brave man who shut the main door, the fire didn't get to the engine room."

Cheers greeted two firefighters when they appeared on deck. Immediately, their blackened faces framed two huge smiles, and they waved. Jeff saw tears falling among smiles as a hundred hugs were passed around.

"The fire was in the storage room right outside the engine room," the captain spoke again. "If it had gotten inside, we would have been in trouble. Once again, God protected us. Thanks for your prayers. You may go back to your cabins."

Everyone roared their approval.

Jeff watched the happy crew and staff disappear. Staring into the cobalt blue water, he studied the surface. Suddenly, he spotted a dozen silvery streaks that flew out of the water and through the air as if they had wings. Startled, Jeff's blue eyes followed them for six or eight feet before they plopped back into the ocean.

"Flying fish!" he yelled, pointing.

With his arms resting on the railing, Jeff took a deep breath. He was in awe of God, who had thought to make fish that could fly. Others gathered around.

"Wahoo!" K.J. whooped. "I knew there was a reason I brought this camera with me!"

He'd already had the camcorder out to get shots of the firemen. Now he turned it toward the ocean. He handed Mindy the still camera.

Studying the waves, Jeff was soon surprised again. Something bumpy and gray gracefully surfaced. A whale! Like a volcano erupting, it sent a mist 20 feet into the air. Jeff guessed the whale's body must be as long as six cars parked bumper to bumper.

Finally, as if waving goodbye, the whale flipped its tail flukes and disappeared. Jeff laughed out loud.

"What footage!" K.J. yelled.

Jeff turned to Michelle. She still stood there in her pink nightshirt, but a grin covered her face.

Jeff thought how much different Michelle was than most girls he knew. He admired her concern for others. She hadn't stopped to grab anything or fix her hair before she came to wake them. People were more important to her than the way she looked.

Jeff's thoughts returned to the fire. He faced Michelle. "Was the fire started in the room we visited last night?"

"That's right," Michelle declared.

"How long will it take to assess the damage?" K.J. asked.

"At least an hour or two, I think," Michelle said.

"I think I'm ready for a shower and some breakfast," Mindy said. "This wind blowing hair in my face is driving me nuts."

❖❖❖❖❖❖❖

In the bathroom down the hall, the boys took turns in the shower. K.J. returned in record time.

"Are you having the same problem I'm having?"

Jeff asked, watching K.J. put his dirty clothes away.

"You mean bumping into the walls in the shower? Yeah. How do these sailors stay on their feet?"

Jeff laughed. "I'm glad I'm not the only one! I keep thinking I'll fall and knock myself out, then someone will have to come and find me. I think it's just hard to stand still while the ship's moving."

They raced down the stairs to the meet the girls on the promenade deck, but Jeff's mind was on Warren. He debated about sharing his dream with the club and finally decided to tell them everything.

When he was nearly finished, he noticed Michelle's eyebrows.

"What's wrong?" Jeff asked. "Did I say something wrong?"

Michelle took a deep breath, biting her lower lip. "You have no idea how significant this is. You know that pole you described? Every voodoo temple has one in the middle."

"I don't want to hear any more," Mindy said, holding her stomach.

"It's okay, Mindy. God is greater than any voodoo." Michelle rubbed her chin.

"And the bright light?"

"It must be God's power," Jeff said.

"Probably. But the light got brighter and brighter," Michelle observed. "Maybe the Lord is giving us the key to breaking the satanic power that has controlled my island for centuries."

"That would be cool," K.J. said. "I'm into war—especially when we know who's going to win!"

Everyone laughed, except Jeff. He couldn't jar Michelle's words from his mind.

❖❖❖❖❖❖❖

At lunchtime, everyone gathered in the main cafeteria. There were not only the ham and cheese sandwiches and salad, but decorations as well. Pressed white tablecloths and floral displays adorned every table.

Jeff admired the way Mission International did things. Everything had an elegance to it, but it was elegance with simplicity. Class, his mother would call it.

Asking for the salad bowl, K.J. broke into his thoughts. The roar of the happy ship crew filled the room. As he put his napkin down, Jeff saw Captain Davidson and Dan enter the room.

When they walked directly to the front, the room hushed. The team was as hungry for details as they'd been for lunch.

Dan smiled at the crowd. "We're fortunate the way things came out. The fire only damaged one storage room. It destroyed a few engine parts and some supplies. Nothing critical to the operation of the ship. The crew is already clearing the rubbish."

Jeff leaned forward as Captain Davidson spoke. "We now know that the source of the fire was a short in an electrical panel. None of our electricians have worked on that panel recently. If you have any knowledge of the situation, please speak to us. Praise God everyone is safe."

Jeff sat back, not able to shake the captain's words. He felt sure someone had tampered with the wires. Dr. Simpson? He surveyed the room, but he didn't see him anywhere.

After lunch, the team returned to the deck. The ship was moving at full speed. Jeff gazed out over the vast ocean. He didn't like what he saw.

Dark clouds had formed. Very dark. The gloomy skies looked like they were going to let loose a terrible storm.

Jeff remembered the captain's words.

Chapter 5

Haiti

Soon, a crowd was eyeing the gathering clouds. Jeff spotted Dan hustling toward the captain's bridge.

"How's it going, Dan?" Jeff asked.

"We'll be in Haiti in a few hours. But it looks like we're not going to escape the hurricane."

"We're praying up a storm," Jeff said.

Dan laughed as he hurried past. "Don't do that!" he said over his shoulder.

Jeff turned red but laughed with the rest of the team.

The clouds grew closer. And darker still. Suddenly, rain started pelting the ship. A violent flash of lightning slashed through the sky. The wind howled. A small table and a couple of empty lawn chairs went skittering across the deck.

The crew raced to tie things down. Everyone else bounded for the safety of the dining area. Jeff and the others followed.

Jeff grunted at Mindy. "I'm too tired to pray, but it seems we've got another battle on our hands."

The waves pounded, bobbing the ship up and down. Water splashed higher and higher against the portholes.

"Oh no," Jeff cried. "Here goes my stomach again."

K.J. flopped into a chair. "I'm going to my cabin and lie down before...you know."

Mindy and Michelle smiled and shook their heads.

Suddenly, Jeff sensed faith rising in his soul. Instantly, his stomach calmed. "Hey. Something's happening to me. Let's pray against this storm. I'm not going to get sick! And we're not going to be delayed any more!"

"Can we hurry?" K.J. said. "I'll throw up soon if I don't get to my bunk."

They grasped hands and Jeff prayed forcefully. "Lord. We're not giving up on Your power. Silence this storm like You did the day You walked on water with the disciples. Drive it back out to sea."

Everyone agreed, but there was no change. Jeff couldn't take any more. His energy was drained. He and K.J. stumbled to their cabin and fell into their bunks. Discouragement mingled with his seasickness.

But after only a few moments, he felt calm. All was quiet. Even the wind stopped whistling. Jeff raised off the bunk to look through the porthole. Bright sunlight was all he could see.

"K.J.," Jeff cried, "God has answered our prayers!"

"Na. Let me look," K.J. said, elbowing Jeff aside.

The boys raced up the stairs. On the deck, astonished crew members stood in groups, looking heavenward. Jeff spotted Michelle and Mindy sitting near the pool. As he scanned the horizon, he saw that blue skies had pushed the clouds away.

Looking toward the bow of the ship, Jeff stared in unbelief. He looked back to the stern.

A large rainbow had appeared all around them.

Mindy pointed, gasping. "It's making a circle around us."

"That's incredible!" Michelle cried. "It looks like God's putting His arms around the ship."

Everyone rejoiced with laughter. K.J. and Michelle raced for their camcorders. Grinning toward the rainbow, Jeff noticed Dr. Simpson a few feet away, looking bewildered. Jeff was afraid to approach him, but he decided to try to make friends with him. Hoping it was the right time, he and Mindy walked over to the doctor.

"Dr. Simpson," Jeff began, "are you feeling better about our trip to Haiti?"

"Not really. And you're probably going to tell me the rainbow is a sign."

Jeff ignored his comment. "What made you come on this trip? Didn't you know the kind of mission we're on?"

Dr. Simpson huffed. "It's definitely not what I thought it would be," he muttered. "I've always wanted to help people. That's why I signed up on the standby list. But I didn't know everybody was so religious."

"Does that bother you?" Mindy asked cautiously.

"I hate religion. I had enough church in my youth. All I saw was hypocrisy, phoniness, and unreality. You know, weird TV evangelists and preachers asking for money."

Jeff managed a nod.

"I'm waiting for that stuff to happen here," the doctor confided. "But so far everyone has kept it hidden."

"That's why we call ourselves the Reel Kids," Jeff said, shielding his eyes from the sun. "We're sick of phoniness in church too. We want the real thing."

"The church has done nothing but fail me," Dr. Simpson snapped. "And if I hang around with you guys long enough, you'll fail me too."

"You're right," Jeff admitted. "That's why you should put your trust in God, not in people. People always fail."

Jeff drew a deep breath, about to continue. Suddenly, he spotted land! "Do you guys see that?" Jeff cried, pointing.

Everyone ran to the bow of the ship.

"That's beautiful!" Mindy cried.

An announcement echoed over the loudspeaker. "This is your captain speaking. Haiti is straight ahead. We'll be there in a couple of hours."

Jeff looked at his watch. "Or seventeen-hundred hours," he smiled, turning back to finish his talk with Dr. Simpson. But the doctor was gone. Jeff looked around, feeling sad because it seemed he was getting somewhere with the man.

Michelle and K.J. ran up, breathing hard.

"It won't be long now," Michelle said.

"Yeah," Mindy said. "I'll bet you have mixed feelings about coming back."

Michelle nodded while she caught her breath.

"Didn't Columbus discover Haiti before America?" Jeff asked.

"That's a long story."

"Can you tell us a little?" Mindy prodded. "We've got some time."

"Okay," Michelle said, leaning on the railing. "I'll share a few things. But we'll be there soon, and it'll be more fun to show you."

"If these new people let us land," K.J. said.

Michelle bit her lower lip as she looked toward Haiti. "You can't imagine what happened here in 1492. After Christopher Columbus discovered Haiti, he founded the first Spanish settlement."

"Was anybody living here at the time?" K.J. asked.

"Yes. Indians. But settlers came in and killed them off."

"Sad. That happened in lots of places, didn't it?" Jeff commented. "What happened next?"

Michelle licked her lips and began. "Finally the French came. When France defeated Spain in Europe, a new treaty gave them total rights to Haiti."

"It must have been beautiful then," Jeff said.

Michelle smiled wistfully. "I'm told it was a tropical paradise. Spectacular mountain ranges, coffee trees, and rolling plains of green sugar cane. Lots of fruit trees. It was France's richest colony."

"What changed that?" Jeff wanted to know. Then he noticed Michelle's sudden embarrassment. "What's wrong?" he asked gently. "Did I say the wrong thing?"

Michelle hesitated, then looked up. "No. It's not you. It's just hard for me to talk about this."

Mindy patted Michelle's arm and smiled understandingly.

"But I'll tell you anyway," she said slowly. "Haiti became one of the largest slave markets around." She paused. "That's how my ancestors got here. Haitian slaves were overworked and beaten. Because of the horrible treatment and conditions, they sometimes lived only a few months. They were replaced again and again."

No one knew what to say. Jeff felt awkward for bringing it up, but Michelle she went on. "Over one million Africans were killed in the first hundred years."

In unison, everyone's mouths flew open.

"That's horrible!" K.J. choked out. "And probably the reason the slaves made their sacrifice to Satan in 1791. It was their way of fighting back."

"Exactly," Michelle said. "Haiti finally got their independence in 1804, and became the first totally free black nation."

Jeff was trying to process everything he heard. "How many people live here now?"

"Over six million," Michelle reported sadly. "I can't believe so many are crammed into a place the size of the state of Maryland. Some are rich, but most are poor. Light and dark, good and evil. But everyone understands Haiti's cruel history."

"What language do the Haitians speak?" Jeff wanted to stay away from the subject of slavery.

"Creole," Michelle said. "It's a mixture of African and French."

"When you say poor," Mindy asked, "how poor?"

"The average income is three hundred twenty-seven dollars a year."

Everyone stared in disbelief. Michelle paused, looking toward Haiti. A tear crawled down her cheek.

Everyone remained quiet for a long while.

❖❖❖❖❖❖❖

As they got nearer to shore, the captain's voice boomed over the loudspeaker. "We don't know what may happen when we arrive. Please be in prayer."

Jeff searched the shoreline. Tiny huts and villages were scattered about. Seeing the poor areas reminded him of other places he'd visited.

It didn't seem fair that there were poor, hurting people in every country of the world. Their pain and poverty always broke his heart. He knew it broke God's heart as well. As he scanned the troubled landscape, he wondered what had happened to paradise.

Then, roaring out of the harbor, Jeff spotted a blue and white boat coming straight toward them. As it neared, he could see it was about 30 feet long and looked like some kind of military boat. The closer it got, the older the boat looked.

As the boat raced alongside, Jeff noticed a hand-ful of military men bustled on board.

They all carried submachine guns. Suddenly, Jeff felt terrified, and he squinted in disbelief.

The gun barrels were pointed at them!

Chapter 6

Anchored

Jeff turned to Mindy. Her brown eyes filled the frames of her glasses. He put an arm around her and whirled toward Michelle. "Do you think they'll shoot?"

"It doesn't look good," she warned. "Haiti is known for cruelty and violence."

Jeff felt his heartbeat quicken. From the upper deck, he watched the men closely until they were hidden when the boat stopped alongside.

Then he heard the winding sound of the gangway door opening. He watched brown Haitian arms throw giant ropes toward the *Charity II*. Seamen's hands reached out, caught the ropes, and tied them securely.

Jeff waited breathlessly, watching the gangway entrance. He knew it would only be minutes before the military men reached the deck.

One after the other, four hefty Haitian men rushed up the stairs. At this close range, their gun barrels looked bigger than anything Jeff had ever seen. The men started yelling loudly in what Jeff figured was Creole.

Large machetes hung from their belts. Automatically, Jeff's hands were in the air. Everyone else had their hands raised as well. Mindy looked terrified. K.J. was frozen.

Silently, Jeff whispered a quick prayer. Out of the corner of his eye, Jeff noticed Dr. Simpson looked frightened too.

Because one man's uniform was sprinkled with military decorations, Jeff assumed he was in charge. Even though he looked unapproachable, Dan and Captain Davidson greeted the men with nods and smiles.

When he barked out an order in Creole, the soldiers instantly snapped their guns to their sides, took several steps back, and stood at attention.

Jeff listened, wanting to understand. Michelle slipped in closer. Jeff hoped she would translate.

"I'm Major Bennett," the leader snapped at Captain Davidson. "Third in charge of the Haitian army."

To Jeff's surprise, the major spoke English very well.

"We demand to know why you're here," the

major continued. "Who gave you authorization to enter Haitian waters at this time?"

Captain Davidson quickly shuffled through a file of papers he was holding. "This is the letter of invitation from your Haitian government officials." The captain handed a piece of paper to Major Bennett.

Jeff watched as the major studied it carefully. Then the man laughed out loud.

Michelle's face became concerned. Jeff's fingers trembled. The major grinned and tossed the paper back. "These are worthless. We've got a new government. I'm ordering an immediate search of the ship. We have reason to believe you're an American spy ship."

Jeff gasped. Dan's face tightened. Mindy flinched.

"Sir," Dan said gently, "we've come with food and supplies to help hurricane victims. We'd like to take it ashore as soon as possible."

Major Bennett gazed at Dan. "I'm sorry. I have my orders. We will begin the search now. I need to inspect the passports of all your crew and passengers immediately. I'll need a table."

Jeff remembered that shortly after they'd boarded the ship in Los Angles, the ship's purser had collected all their passports. She'd explained that it was her job to keep them in a safe and, when they entered each new country or port, to fill out any necessary paperwork.

Jeff glanced toward Dr. Simpson. He looked red hot, but he didn't say a word.

Night was falling like a slow-moving curtain. With darkness came fear.

Additional soldiers had been called up from the boat to help with the search. Brown uniforms filled the stairs and the decks.

From their spot on the bow, the club heard booted footsteps everywhere. Jeff could tell soldiers were rustling through cabin after cabin. He wondered what he would find when he returned to his cabin.

A special table was set up in the nearby international lounge. Through the window, Jeff could see the purser calmly presenting everyone's passport, one by one. The major seemed to loosen up as they worked together. Jeff couldn't believe the crew. Their attitudes were cooperative and friendly.

"We're in a battle now," he whispered to Mindy. "I think God is trying to teach us something. Big time."

"That's for sure," Mindy sighed. "Let me know when you figure out what it is."

Jeff looked for K.J. and prayed that wherever he was, his camera wasn't running.

❖❖❖❖❖❖❖

After a while, the major appeared on deck again with Dan and Captain Davidson. The team stood by, watching. During a break in the conversation, Michelle grinned at Major Bennett. "Sir, how did you learn to speak English so well?"

He looked at her curiously. "Are you the only Haitian who knows English, young lady?"

Michelle blushed.

Then the major chuckled in a deep resounding sound. "Seriously. An American teacher taught me years ago."

Michelle managed a nod.

"Excuse me," the major said. He turned back to Captain Davidson. "Your ship must stay anchored off shore until further notice."

Captain Davidson nodded, looking surprised. "May I ask why, sir?"

Major Bennett's face turned ice cold. "Simple. Your ship is under arrest."

Chapter 7

Boat People

Jeff felt numb. He didn't believe his ears. "Arrested?" he mumbled. "In the middle of the Caribbean?"

Everyone was stunned. Jeff noticed the calm expressions on Dan and Captain Davidson's faces. Even after this, they didn't get angry or argue.

Immediately, Warren came to Jeff's mind. He guessed Warren had to be in trouble if they were. He wished he could ask Major Bennett, but he didn't dare.

For a moment, he stared into space, then turned to Michelle. "I've got an idea," he whispered.

"Maybe you could ask the major about Warren. I think he likes you."

Michelle nodded reluctantly.

Casually, she strolled closer, then stood still.

When Major Bennett took a breath between sentences, he noticed her. "You're the Haitian onboard, aren't you? The purser told me about you."

"I am, sir," she said faintly. "I left Haiti when I was twelve. My family became American citizens."

Jeff wondered if she'd made a mistake telling the major she was an American citizen. To fight his anxiety, he prayed hard.

Major Bennett chuckled. "Many Haitians are leaving lately. Maybe I should take a hint from all this."

"Sir," she said with a sweet grin, "could I ask you a question?"

When he didn't stop her, she continued. "An American man named Warren Russell landed at the airport yesterday from Los Angeles. Would you have any idea what happened to him?"

Major Bennett paused. Then he laughed out loud. "You know, Michelle. I like you. You're a bold girl. Maybe you should work for us."

Michelle laughed a little. Jeff had been hoping for an answer, but the major seemed to be flirting with her. Major Bennett stopped grinning, though, when he noticed the serious expression on her face. "Well, I can tell you no Americans have been killed. But all foreigners have been put under arrest for twenty-four hours. Since we haven't arrested all enemy Haitians, our city is very unstable."

"Thank you," Michelle said, nodding and backing off.

Major Bennett turned and bellowed some orders in Creole. Then he departed quickly with two of his soldiers. With rifles over their shoulders and ammunition hanging from their belts, the others remained on board.

❖❖❖❖❖❖❖

The first gleam of daylight shot through the boys' porthole on Thursday morning. It was seven o'clock when Jeff woke. An hour before breakfast.

Listening to K.J. snore, Jeff wondered what would happen to them now.

He crawled out of his bunk, flopped into the cabin chair, and opened his Bible. Yawning, he turned to his daily devotions.

Jeff read a verse in Ephesians 6. "We wrestle not against flesh and blood," it said, "but against principalities and powers, and the ruler of the darkness."

The words shocked him. His dream came flooding back. In his mind, he pictured the slithering snake. He knew God wanted to show him something.

Thinking about the bright light that drove the snake away, Jeff realized that he—the whole ship, in fact—was captive to the Haitian government. And in some way he didn't fully understand, captives of the snake as well. Chills raced up his spine.

❖❖❖❖❖❖❖

After Jeff dressed, he strolled along the Promenade deck. He agonized over being stuck again, just like in Panama. This whole trip seemed to be one brick wall after another.

He wrestled with his thoughts, trying to discover the key to defeating the snake. He knew God was bigger than the major and voodoo power, but he still felt helpless.

Deciding to eat, he headed for the cafeteria. Walking over to the table, he couldn't believe his eyes.

Dr. Simpson was sitting with the same volunteers he'd had in the room with him the other night. Glancing at them, Jeff noticed their angry expressions. He felt fearful, but he didn't know what to do.

Before he could figure it out, Mindy, K.J., and Michelle came in and found a table. After loading a plate with orange slices, toast, and a bowl of oatmeal, Jeff joined them.

"I think Dr. Simpson is causing more trouble than the Haitian government," he said as he sat down.

Everyone glanced toward the doctor. Jeff knew it was none of his business, but he felt he had to do something. Boldly, he rose from his breakfast, walked over to the one empty seat at the doctor's table, and sat down. He was afraid his heart might jump out of his chest.

Immediately, he remembered the verse from the Bible. "We wrestle not against flesh and blood."

Jeff sucked in a deep breath. One at a time, he looked the other volunteers in the eye. Then he faced Dr. Simpson. "I know you're upset at all that's happened."

First Dr. Simpson chuckled, then he groaned. He looked like a volcano ready to explode.

"Look." Jeff wasn't going to quit now. "This has been hard for everybody. I haven't seen this kind of spiritual warfare before."

"Spiritual warfare!" Dr. Simpson scoffed. "This is stupidity! The captain knows better. I warned them not to come here. Now just look what they've got us into!"

Jeff felt speechless. He anxiously leaned closer. "It's bad enough for the military to be against us. But it's really bad when we're fighting among ourselves. We have to trust Captain Davidson and Dan. They'll do what's best."

Jeff waited, not taking his eyes off the group.

Dr. Simpson raised his nose in the air and laughed. "I know what I'm doing. I'm getting off this ship as soon as possible. And so are these people," he said with a dramatic sweep of his hand.

Jeff felt his anger surge, wondering if he was helping. Then he remembered the verse again: "We wrestle not against flesh and blood, but against principalities and powers."

He aimed his gaze at the volunteers. "How many of you are believers?"

They glanced around and looked at each other a moment. Then one man raised his hand. Slowly, the others did too.

Jeff leaned back. "I don't think our leaders made a mistake coming to Haiti. We're in the middle of a spiritual war. The fight is not with people, but with Satan. We all need to make sure we're on the right side."

Jeff took a deep breath. The words were flowing, and he could feel God helping him.

The volunteers nodded attentively. Dr. Simpson rolled his eyes, but Jeff determined to keep on. He told the group at the table about his dream. Before he got to the end, Dr. Simpson burst from his seat, mumbling something about more breakfast.

Jeff knew he had to talk fast. His goal was to change the volunteers' allegiance from Dr. Simpson to God. They all agreed to pray about who was right. Jeff thanked them for listening and rejoined Mindy, K.J., and Michelle.

❖❖❖❖❖❖❖

From the deck, Jeff saw the wide bay of Port-au-Prince. Dan had asked the crew to gather in small groups to pray. Wiping sweat from his neck made Jeff realize how hot and humid it was, but he tried to stay focused.

"What's wrong?" Jeff whispered when he noticed tears in Michelle's eyes.

She shook her head, then burst into sobs. While Mindy comforted her, Jeff mopped his brow. Finally, Michelle calmed down.

"Do you want to talk about it?" Jeff asked her.

Michelle wiped her eyes, embarrassed by her tears. "I'll be all right. It's just that seeing Port-au-Prince brings back bad memories."

"I'll bet," Mindy said, putting her arm around her.

Jeff scanned Haiti's troubled capital city. Thick, white-walled colonial buildings looked like they were climbing the surrounding hills.

Michelle pointed to a crowded, dirty-looking

area. "Over there is one of the poorest districts. That's where my family lived."

Jeff closed one eye and peered through the zoom lens of K.J.'s camera. He could see people moving around broken-down shacks and mud huts. Children were playing in the streets.

"There's unimaginable poverty there." Michelle inhaled deeply. "That area is called Croix-des-Missions. It's always been poor. Lots of crime. My homeland is one of the poorest nations in the world."

Everyone strained to see what she described.

"I can only imagine what the hurricane did." Michelle blinked back tears. "That area has always been crowded with huts. They build them out of boxes, mud, straw, tin strips—whatever they can find. Of course they were destroyed."

"Aren't there any decent building materials?" K.J. wanted to know.

"Some are made of cinder block. There are no toilets, no jobs, no work. In one area, the raw sewage runs right down the middle of the street into a stream."

Everyone gulped. Mindy closed her eyes tightly.

"There's much starvation," Michelle spoke softly. "Children often lay on the ground with swollen bellies and frizzy reddish hair."

"Why does their hair turn red?" Mindy asked, holding back tears.

"It happens to black children who don't get enough protein. The kids become very depressed. Then they develop severe brain damage. Death must be a relief to them."

Jeff's heart felt like it was about to explode. "Why don't we pray?"

❖❖❖❖❖❖❖

After a while, Jeff looked up. His mind ticked through a million questions. He knew Mindy had them too. K.J. was running his camcorder, though being extremely careful since the soldiers were still there.

Jeff turned to Michelle. "What do Haitians normally eat?"

"If they eat at all, it's usually rice and beans. Maybe bananas, mangoes, or some other tropical fruit. An occasional chicken. On a great holiday, they eat pork."

Everyone looked at each other, contemplating.

"Boy," K.J. moaned. "We have it made. I can't imagine only eating rice and beans everyday."

"Do they have stoves?" Mindy asked.

Michelle laughed. "Haitians cook on outdoor fires. And get their water from open ditches."

Jeff was confused. How could there be so much wealth and food in some parts of the world and so little in others? He felt helpless again. He felt compassion for people who lived with so little.

"Now that part of Haiti is totally different." Michelle pointed to another location. "Those people don't eat rice and beans."

"What do you mean?" Mindy asked.

"That's the suburbs. It's called Petionville. The Beverly Hills of Haiti."

Jeff focused the zoom lens on the area. Even

though he could barely see it, he noticed an obvious difference.

Michelle became tearful. "The millionaires of Haiti live there. There's always been a war between rich and poor. Between light-skinned and dark. Between the church and the military."

"What do you mean?" Mindy scratched her head, looking confused.

"Well," Michelle said, "the Mulatto Haitians are light-skinned—a mix of white and black. They're usually the ruling class. But since their government just got kicked out, they must be worried."

Everyone focused toward the direction of Petionville.

"In Petionville and some other suburbs," Michelle continued, "the rich have built fancy mansions. Little outposts of luxury. The homes are surrounded by walls. And the walls are topped with broken glass and barbed wire to keep anyone from climbing over. Inside, they have lots of servants."

"How much danger are the rich in now?" Jeff asked.

"Some will be killed," Michelle admitted. "But soon, another government backing the rich will take over. It goes back and forth. The one thing that never changes is that the poor are always the ones who suffer."

The sun was straight overhead, and it was getting hotter by the moment.

Wiping his brow, Jeff gasped as he stood up. "What's happening?"

Michelle rose quickly to get a better look. Crew members gathered along the railing to stare toward the harbor. Heading out to sea were a dozen or so broken-down boats.

"Where are they going?" Mindy cried.

Michelle bit her lip. "I don't know. Probably to the shores of Miami. That's five hundred miles from here. Every time there's a coup, hundreds flee Haiti on boats like that."

Jeff had heard of boat people but had never seen them. He knew their overcrowded, makeshift boats often capsized, leaving many drowned. It made him afraid for the people who were headed out of the harbor. Suddenly, it hit him what was happening.

"They're not going to Miami!" he exclaimed. "They're coming toward us!"

Chapter 8

Port–au–Prince

"How many boats are there?" Jeff watched in amazement.

Everyone counted, hurriedly. K.J. flipped in a new video. He whirled the camera around and raised it to his eye. "I got eighteen," he said, peering into the lens.

"Hey, this reminds me, K.J.," Jeff said. "When Dr. Simpson insisted you erase that tape. Did you?"

"Well...," he said with a sly smile, "sometimes I'm not exactly sure how this camera works. I think I may still have a small piece of his little mutiny speech."

Jeff chuckled and shook his head. Suddenly, he heard a soldier yelling and running toward them. K.J. jerked the camcorder down. Jeff hoped they wouldn't confiscate it.

When the soldiers reached the railing, the boats were bobbing closer and closer. Jeff couldn't believe they could float. They were each crammed with more bodies than he'd seen in such a small space. Some weren't even real boats. They were rafts made from broken pieces of wood, metal, and string. Yet they somehow stayed afloat.

Jeff studied the Haitian faces. Their desperate expressions said it all—fear, anxiety, despair. Jeff knew they wanted out. He was sure the brightly painted *Charity II* looked like the perfect answer to them.

When the lead boat was ready to toss a line to the ship, one of the soldiers raised his gun and aimed. Jeff stood on his tiptoes then held back. The soldiers were about to shoot innocent men, women, and children!

A shot rang out. Jeff's eyes widened to see if anyone was hit. Then another shot pierced the air. He felt helpless.

Looking at the bobbing, overloaded boats, Jeff saw an older man holding his arm. Blood was flowing from a shoulder wound.

Jeff turned to Michelle in panic. There was terror on her face. But instead of running away, she ran to the soldier. Crying, she pleaded with him. Jeff didn't understand Creole, but he knew she was begging them to stop.

Jeff watched and prayed.

Finally, the soldier slowly lowered his gun.

Captain Davidson and Dan appeared from inside and stared in disbelief. Jeff wondered if they'd faced anything this horrible before.

Glancing toward the harbor, Jeff saw three military boats speeding their direction. Dozens of men in brown uniforms were lining up along the decks. Their guns were raised.

"They're going to kill them!" Mindy cried, covering her eyes.

Holding his camera casually at his side, K.J. got it all on tape.

Jeff peeked over the side. The companionway, which attaches to the ship at anchor to accomodate launches, was still up. He knew Dan and Captain Davidson had to make a decision.

If they opened the gangway entrance, the ship would be overrun with desperate Haitians. If they didn't, the Haitians would be killed.

Jeff's heart leapt in his chest. The verse came back into his mind. This battle was not between people. It was a battle of the forces of hell trying to destroy their mission and kill hundreds of Haitians.

Jeff leaned over the side. Haitians tried desperately to find something to tie their boats to. It would be only seconds before the military boats arrived.

In the lead military boat, he saw a familiar face—Major Bennett. Standing along the railing, Dan and Captain Davidson saw him too. The Haitian boats were pushed back by the military boats so the gangway could be opened.

To his relief, the soldiers held their fire. One by one, the military boats pushed the shoddy boats away from the ship. With the screech of scraping metal, the companionway was opened. Major Bennett's boat docked.

Jeff heard the voice on the loudspeaker. "Please clear the gangway. Major Bennett is coming aboard."

As Jeff leaned over, the gangway slowly opened up. Jeff prayed hard. He was sure the entire crew was praying along with him.

Moments later, Major Bennett strode up the stairs. Though he still looked angry, Jeff watched the cordial way Dan and Captain Davidson greeted him. Still praying, Jeff was hanging on every word.

Everyone aboard was silent. The only thing Jeff heard were the faint cries that drifted up from the boat people.

"Your ship is causing much grief," Major Bennett said, looking Captain Davidson in the eye. "The only choice I have is to send you back to America."

Jeff's heart sank. Dan and Captain Davidson didn't say anything.

Slowly, Major Bennett strolled to the rail. He looked over the side as if he was deep in thought. Finally, he turned back. His voice dropped in pitch. "But if I send you away, those boats will follow you."

Major Bennett rubbed his chin. Jeff could tell he was making a very important decision. "Many will die," he said with a long sigh. "I'm tired of death and destruction. That's all I've known on Haiti. Death. From rotten leaders. From hurricanes. I'm sick of it."

Michelle's eyes filled with tears.

The major quickly noticed her and smiled eagerly. "I wish all Haitians were like you."

Michelle grinned through her tears. Then the major paused again and turned to the captain. "I've decided to change my mind."

Jeff prayed intensely. He didn't want to hear bad news.

"I'm going to let your ship dock in the harbor," the major went on.

Suddenly, Jeff's being burst with new energy. God's light was beginning to defeat the snake.

"And because of my people and their need after the hurricane, I'm even going to allow you to unload your food and supplies. And if I don't hear of any trouble, maybe your teams can go into the villages— on a day-to-day basis."

Disbelief and joy filled Jeff's heart. He forced himself not to cartwheel across the deck.

Dan smiled cautiously at Major Bennett. "Thank you, sir," he said with his eyes as well as his words. He extended his hand to the major. "Perhaps you can offer protection for our teams?"

Major Bennett managed a slight smile and a nod. "Of course our soldiers will keep an eye on you."

Jeff wanted to jump into the air. Mindy and K.J. still had their mouths open. Tears flooded down Michelle's face.

Major Bennett's face suddenly changed. A serious look. "Remember, you're still under investigation. But in the meantime, our people can really use your help."

❖❖❖❖❖❖❖

It was four in the afternoon when the ship finally docked in Port-au-Prince. Though thankful for the major's change of heart, Jeff was still anxious to find out what had happened to Warren.

In spite of the military herding the boat people onto shore like cattle, no one had been seriously hurt. The ship's medical personal removed the bullet from the man who had been shot. They said he would recover nicely.

From the deck, Jeff surveyed the damage Hurricane Audrey had inflicted upon Port-au-Prince. Roofs were blown off houses. Everywhere, shacks and mud huts were flattened. Trash floated in the water and was strewn across the harbor. They had heard many of the dead were already buried.

Jeff wanted to go ashore immediately, but Dan's orders were to secure the ship. A strategy meeting would be held before anyone could leave the boat, he'd said.

❖❖❖❖❖❖❖

Thursday afternoon was disappearing into the sunset by the time they got off the ship. Dan had ordered everyone to stay in the dock area until Friday, when they were scheduled to take supplies into the villages. Jeff was dying to know if Warren was okay.

On the dock, Jeff glanced about. Beggars lined the wharf. Hungry Haitians held containers and waited for food. Little children hung on tired mothers. Desperation filled everyone's eyes. Jeff's heart was stirred with compassion.

Suddenly, his heart leapt. Straining his eyes down the harbor road, he looked closer. He rubbed his eyes in disbelief. In the distance, he saw Warren dodging his way through the crowd.

Jeff started toward him but quickly remembered Dan's orders. Then K.J. and Mindy spotted Warren too. Jumping for joy and spinning around, they couldn't wait to see their leader. Jeff was grateful he was safe.

Warren was soon close enough for Jeff to see the gigantic smile on Warren's face. As always, his soft, brown eyes flickered with warmth. He was an inch taller than Jeff, but they had the same medium build. His sandy-brown hair was short enough to qualify him for Major Bennett's military troops. Running down the crowded dock, he looked energetic enough as well.

Though it was still hot, he wore blue chinos and a blue and red plaid shirt. Jeff chuckled when he noticed that Warren wasn't wearing socks with his loafers. Warren was in his early thirties, but he was often mistaken for one of the students. It probably didn't help, Jeff thought, that the team called him by his first name when they were away from school.

"Boy, are we glad to see you!" Jeff cried when Warren was within shouting distance.

"Me too," Warren said with a grin. "I heard about your arrival. Everyone in Port-au-Prince is aware of the ship."

"Yeah," K.J. said with a laugh. "We had half of Haiti trying to get aboard."

Warren chuckled, hugging everyone.

"Are you okay, Warren?" Mindy asked.

"You won't believe it," Warren replied. "My plane was early. The coup went into action two hours after I arrived. After the team picked me up from the airport and took me to the house, it all broke loose. Until an hour ago, we were under house arrest."

Everyone took turns sharing stories of the voyage, talking and laughing all at once.

After they finished, Warren turned to Jeff. "Where is Captain Davidson? And Dan?"

Jeff pointed toward the ship. "They're working to get teams out tomorrow. But they'll be glad to see you."

"I'd better check in with them," Warren said. "You guys stay close to the ship. Bullets are still flying around here."

Jeff didn't want to hear that. Neither did Mindy.

Strolling along the maze of docks, Jeff was grateful to finally be in Haiti. He knew they were in the right place.

Suddenly, Michelle looked frightened. Jeff moved to her side. "What's wrong, Michelle?" he asked.

Michelle turned toward him. Quietly, she nodded to a middle-aged man with a chocolate ice cream cone in his hand. Beside him, an eleven- or twelve-year-old girl licked a cone of her own.

"That man," Michelle whispered. "He's probably the most well-known voodoo priest in Haiti. I remember him from when I was little. That must be his daughter."

Jeff's eyebrows raised higher as the pair came closer. To his shock, they stopped right in front of the club. By now, Mindy and K.J. were watching them too.

The man didn't look the way Jeff expected a voodoo priest to look. He was no taller than K.J. and dressed in plain blue jeans and a black polo shirt.

The girl looked like any other Haitian kid, although she wasn't as skinny. Her shorts and t-shirt were as dirty as all the others on the dock, and short, black curls framed her rounded face, giving her an impish quality.

The man stared at each club member one after the other. At first, Jeff didn't feel afraid. But the priest's eyes were strange, like they looked right through him.

Jeff caught a glimpse of embroidery on his shirt. He gasped when he realized what it was—a snake slithering down a pole.

An icy chill began at the nape of his neck and crept, like a snake, all the way down his back.

The priest leaned closer. "My name is Francis Boudier. This is my daughter, Maxine."

The girl's wide, black eyes narrowed in a dirty look.

"Excuse me, dear," he said to her, clearing his throat. "She likes to be called Max. Anyway, we understand your ship is here to help our people."

Jeff and Michelle both nodded, impressed with how well Francis spoke English.

The pupils of Francis's eyes became dark. Very dark. "We welcome any help," he said. "But..."

Jeff rocked back on his heels.

"...don't attempt to interfere with our religious beliefs."

Jeff gulped.

The priest moved closer still. "If you do, you'll suffer horrible consequences."

Chapter 9

Voodoo

Jeff was speechless. He'd never met a voodoo priest. It was almost as if evil pulsated from him.

Max snickered, enjoying the warning her father had given, but Jeff didn't feel any evil coming from the girl. Jeff wished for a second that Max could be part of their club.

Then the priest looked at Michelle. "You're a native Haitian, aren't you? You left here years ago. I can see you've been deceived by Americans."

Jeff's eyes widened. Michelle's face tightened, and she looked terrified. Jeff wondered how the voodoo priest knew anything about her.

Without another word, the priest and his young daughter disappeared into the crowd. Jeff turned to Michelle. Everyone stood in silence.

Shaken, the team returned to the ship to pray against the power of the voodoo priest. They knew God was greater.

An hour later, everyone gathered for a meeting. Hearing plans to help the Haitian people filled Jeff with energy. And to Jeff's amazement, even Dr. Simpson was there.

❖❖❖❖❖❖❖

The club's first assignment on Friday morning was to travel with a prayer team. Jeff was overjoyed when he heard the ship always prepared for their ministry by sending prayer teams out.

As they prepared to go, Warren and Michelle joined them. Michelle would be their guide.

❖❖❖❖❖❖❖

Stumbling down the rugged road, Jeff was caught off-guard by the sights. Dirty, naked kids played everywhere. Their coffee-colored skin was grayed with dust.

Jeff heard a strange mix of sounds—chirping birds and leaves blowing in the wind, then splashing water and a pounding sound.

Looking toward a small stream, he saw Haitians sitting on the slopes, flopping clothes against rocks in the filthy stream. Burros wallowed in the same water. *They must be washing their clothes*, Jeff thought.

With tears in her eyes, Michelle watched too. "This district is called La Saline. It's one of the most densely populated and poorest places in the world, almost as bad as Cite Soceil."

Michelle paused. "I had an aunt who lived here once. She was my last relative in Haiti, but she died two years ago. It makes me sad to think this was my home and now there isn't even anyone left here to visit."

Jeff eyed houses, entire settlements, made of cardboard packing boxes. Huts looked thrown together out of random hunks of wood or metal. He wasn't sure if things had always looked this way or if the hurricane had done the damage.

The people looked sadly malnourished. There was no food, no water, not enough land. They had no possessions and nothing to do with their time. Filth was everywhere. A buzzing layer of insects covered it all.

Privacy was rare. Barefoot crowds of beggars, children, peddlers, shoeshine boys, babies, herdsman, travelers, farmers, thieves, and police conducted their business along these roads.

Warren walked alongside Jeff, praying as they walked. Moving higher up the mountain, the evidence of the hurricane became obvious. People desperately needed to rebuild their devastated lives.

The team stopped along the way. Ahead, Jeff saw something that made him gasp. "What is that?"

Michelle looked in the direction Jeff was pointing. "A voodoo temple."

Jeff moved closer, his heart beating fast.

"It's huge," Mindy cried, taking it all in.

Again, Jeff gasped. "Look! That's the pole I saw in my dream. The very same!"

Michelle nodded with a big grin. "There are lots of temples like this. They're called peristyles. The pole in the middle is painted with spiraled serpents."

Jeff was speechless as Michelle went on. "They hold meetings every night. Sometimes in the daytime too. Those drums you see are used to call spirits forth."

Jeff shivered. His skin felt crawly—like he was too close to the evil snake.

Warren looked around. "I heard some amazing stories from the team I stayed with. There are some evil powers here."

"Let's have a prayer meeting right now," Michelle suggested.

K.J.'s eyes about popped out. "Right here? What if a voodoo priest sees us?"

"We'll be okay," Michelle said. "That's what we're supposed to be doing today. Let's go over there."

Everyone crept closer to the temple.

"People are very superstitious," Michelle said faintly. "They'll do anything to please the spirits, including putting lizards and things in a cage to keep bad spirits away. Haitians believe spirits create werewolves, and spooks."

Mindy's eyes got bigger than ever. "I don't understand," she said. "But I'm not sure I want to."

Everyone stood silent for a moment.

Jeff tried to piece things together. Finally, his face lit up. "No wonder I had that dream! God is trying to expose the evil power here. But His power is greater."

"Well," Mindy tried hard to smile, "I'm glad I'm on the right team."

❖❖❖❖❖❖❖

As the club made their way back to the ship, Jeff's mind was going a mile a minute. Though they'd had a powerful prayer time at the voodoo temple, he still hadn't figured out the meaning of his dream.

Suddenly Mindy screamed.

"What's wrong?" Jeff yelled. "What is it?"

With a horrified expression on her face, Mindy pointed to the wooden post directly in front of the ship's gangway. "It's a bottle. But look inside! Yuck! There's the head of a chicken in there!"

"What does that mean?" Warren asked.

Michelle moved closer. "I'd bet the voodoo priest did it."

"What do you mean?" Mindy cried.

"He's put a curse on us."

Chapter 10

Wounded

"What will happen to us?" K.J. looked concerned.

Michelle laughed, though Jeff saw her lower lip trembling. "I doubt anyone considers us anywhere near important enough to curse," she said. "The priest probably just put it here to scare us."

"God's power is greater than any ol' chicken head." Warren smiled reassuringly. "Jesus shed His blood to destroy evil and darkness."

"Can we pray?" Mindy asked with a shaky voice.

"Great idea, Mindy," Warren agreed. "Let's do it right here. Jeff, would you lead us?"

Jeff eyed the suspicious bottle. "Can we take that thing down first?"

"Sure," Warren said. "But remember. It's only a symbol of a force behind it."

Warren reached up and grabbed it. After tossing it in a pile of garbage on the dock, they joined hands. "Okay. Let's pray."

"Lord Jesus," Jeff began. "Show Your power to the people of Haiti. Right now, I break the power of this curse in Jesus' name. Lord, I pray Your light would shine on Haiti and chase out any darkness. Teach even the voodoo priests about Your love."

Everyone said amen.

❖❖❖❖❖❖❖

After lunch, the ship was like a beehive of activity. Scouting teams returned with reports of new places to minister. Two medical teams were heading out to set up clinics in the villages.

Dr. Simpson gave Jeff a dirty look on his way out with the first team. Jeff and the club stayed on the ship to film the unloading of the cargo.

Jeff's heart nearly burst as he watched the crew pile enormous crates from *Charity II*'s cargo holds onto the dock. Blankets, building supplies, medicines, and food had all been donated to help the Haitian people.

Mindy was so excited she nearly bubbled over. She had been invited to help the hospital staff. Until the clinic opened at three o'clock, she and Michelle helped with the shoot.

As Michelle worked, Mindy turned to her. "Will there be any operations today?"

"Probably not," Michelle replied. "The first thing the staff does is screen people for possible surgeries."

"What do you mean?" Mindy asked. "You don't turn people away, do you?"

"Some," Michelle said. "We help as many as we can, but the need is overwhelming. We do try to handle all the children."

Finally, the club was ready to film the opening of the clinic.

The crowd began gathering long before three o'clock. Jeff saw women holding babies and sick children. Bandaged hurricane victims lined up. Many looked like they were in pain. Most had suffered cuts or broken bones from debris swirling around in hundred-mile-an-hour winds.

Jeff watched the waiting crowd, which grew by the minute. He couldn't believe so many people had heard about the hospital on board.

Small covered pick-up trucks called "tap taps" roared up. Jeff noticed the cheerful scenes and happy mottos painted all over them. One said, "Smile. God loves you."

Weary-looking people filed out of the backs. The men and women were dressed in blue jeans or shorts and t-shirts or blouses. Most were dirty, ragged, and worn. It was obvious to Jeff how poor Haiti was.

The people lined up all the way down the docks and up the streets. As far as Jeff could see, there were people—on foot, on bicycles, even one little boy on a stretcher. Hope filled their weakened eyes.

Many of the children were pale and thin, with reddened hair from lack of nutritious food. At that moment, Jeff was overwhelmed. He felt like they needed 20 ships. He wished he had the power to meet every need.

Jeff was proud of Mindy, who greeted people at a table, ready to help with the paperwork. K.J. and Michelle were busy filming, but she stayed close to translate for Jeff as he talked to people along the line. Jeff was constantly looking for a good story. His goal was excellent footage—good enough for the ship to use to raise money to help others.

The nursing staff moved expertly through the crowd, studying injuries and making notes.

Jeff's eyes froze on a nurse who was speaking to a mother. In her arms, she clutched an infant in a ragged blanket. He could hardly see through the crowd, so he motioned for Michelle and K.J. to follow him.

When he got close enough to see the baby's face, he felt his heart melt. The baby's upper lip looked like it had been pushed up and attached to her nose, leaving a gaping hole where her top teeth would be.

K.J. filmed as the nurse pulled the mother out of line and led them to the table where Mindy was working. Jeff decided to interview Michelle and the mother with the baby on the spot. He shared his idea with Michelle, who asked the mother for permission. Gently, Michelle took the child in her arms and lovingly cradled the baby.

"Today," Jeff said, smiling into the camera, "we're working aboard the mercy ship *Charity II*, which is in Haiti helping hurricane victims."

He turned toward Michelle and the baby. "Michelle, who has been working on the ship for a year, is here with me."

Jeff moved closer. "Michelle, who do we have here?"

Michelle cuddled the baby. Turning the baby around, she showed the baby's face to Jeff and the camera. "Her name is Marie."

Jeff grinned.

"She was born with a cleft lip," Michelle continued. "In a couple of days, Marie will have an operation to correct this birth defect. She'll be able to eat normally and live a normal life."

K.J. turned the camera to the mother, who was weeping.

In a few seconds, K.J. lowered the camera. "We'll get more footage and finish Marie's story after the operation."

Suddenly, everyone was startled by a popping noise. Gunshots. Nearby. Looking over the wharf, Jeff saw a crowd gathering.

"Someone's been shot!" he cried.

"What's new?" K.J. said. "There've been lots of shots the past few days."

"Let's not just stand here," Jeff snapped. "We've got to do something."

"It's dangerous out there," Michelle exclaimed. "We need to be careful."

Jeff ignored them. He knew it was dangerous, but he was a reporter. He had to find out what was going on. Just then, Warren ran out, and Jeff sprang up to meet him. "Warren, someone's been shot out there. Can we check it out?"

Warren paused a moment, biting his lip. "We gotta be careful. There's lots of unrest around here. People have been killed every day."

Jeff stared at Warren, his heart fluttering. "I know it's crazy. But I just feel we need to check this one out."

Warren put his hand on Jeff's shoulder, grinning. "Well, if you feel strongly about it, I'll go with you. That's what Reel Kids is all about. Doing what is right."

Jeff nodded as they headed in the direction of the shots. Mindy, Michelle, and K.J. followed. Jeff hoped Major Bennett's soldiers would be near, just in case.

As Jeff pushed through the crowd, the rest of the team followed right behind him. He gasped when he saw a young girl sprawled on the dirt road. Her leg was bleeding badly. "Haven't I seen her before?" he asked, turning to Michelle. "She looks familiar."

Michelle's hand flew up to cover her mouth.

"Yes," she cried. "It's Max!"

Chapter 11

Accused

Jeff heard what she said, but he couldn't take it in. He was sick at the amount of blood. Though Max was grimacing with pain, her eyes were open wide, and she was crying for help.

"What should we do?" K.J. cried. As if it had a mind of its own, his camera was pointed straight at her.

"We can't leave her here," Jeff said.

Mindy reached down. "Let's take her to the ship. We have doctors who can help."

Everything happened at lightning speed. Warren scooped Max up and headed down the dock.

Michelle ran ahead with Mindy to inform the medical staff of the emergency.

Running the girl up the gangway, Warren was breathing hard. K.J. and his camera ran along beside. Jeff tried not to think that Max might die. He glanced at her crumpled body. He wondered what Max had experienced in her young life.

When they arrived at the top of the gangway, two men waited with a stretcher.

"Put her on this," Michelle cried.

Two nurses ran up and applied pressure to the wound to stop the bleeding. Max was barely conscious.

"Let's pray for her," Jeff insisted.

Michelle nodded. "Sure. But we'll have to hurry."

Quickly, Jeff put his hand on Max's leg. Then he realized again who she was—the voodoo priest's daughter. His mind raced, wondering if God had allowed this to happen.

Before Jeff finished, the men carried little Max off to the ship's hospital. The club followed close behind. A young doctor met them.

"How bad is it?" the doctor asked.

"Bullet to the leg," a nurse quickly replied. "Looks like it did some real damage to the bone. To stop the bleeding, we'll need to remove the bullet immediately."

The doctor asked everyone to wait outside. Slowly, Jeff turned to Michelle. "I can't believe a child her age got shot. She can't be over twelve."

Michelle shook her head slowly in agreement. "The scary thing about stray bullets is that they can hit anyone or anything. But things might get worse when her dad finds out we're helping her."

"He'll be thrilled," Mindy said, rolling her brown eyes.

"That's for sure," Michelle replied. "He doesn't like what we stand for. I just know he's the one who put the chicken head in that bottle."

K.J. looked confused. "This whole thing is amazing," he said. "The voodoo priest puts a curse on us. Then his daughter is shot a block away from us."

"Yeah." Jeff suddenly understood what K.J. said. "I think God's trying to show us something. Maybe He's trying to show her dad the truth."

An hour passed. After getting a quick bite in the dining room, the club headed back to the hospital ward to wait some more.

Finally, the doctor walked out. He was smiling. "The operation was a success. She's going to be fine. The bullet did shatter the bone, so we had to cast the leg. But it also just missed an artery. If it had hit there, she might've bled to death. Good thing you brought her in when you did."

The doctor looked up at the clock. "It's six-thirty, and she just woke up. She told me she was staying with her grandmother. She'd sent her to the docks to buy a fish for dinner. Max won't be able to go home tonight. Someone needs to contact her family."

"Someone may have told them by now," Jeff said.

"I'm sure if anyone had told Francis, he'd be here by now," the doctor remarked dryly.

Jeff stared at Michelle. Her eyelids shot up like a rocket. She was grinning as if they both were on the same thought wave.

"Oh, boy. I know what you're thinking," Michelle said. "But maybe we should send somebody else. Francis is pretty scary. I'd have to ask someone where he lives, but that shouldn't be hard. Everyone in Port-au-Prince knows him."

Jeff scratched his head in frustration. Then he turned to Warren. "Maybe we should find him?"

Warren smiled. "Okay. Okay. I'll go with you. But somebody needs to stay with Max."

Mindy smiled. "K.J. and I will stay."

❖❖❖❖❖❖❖

Darkness fell fast. Jeff, Michelle, and Warren hurried down the bustling, crowded street. Jeff heard drums thumping and throbbing from the ravines and hills intersecting Port-au-Prince.

Mingled with those noises were the nagging sounds of barking dogs and the cooing, cackling, and crowing of birds and chickens.

They passed shoe-shine boys who beat their boxes like drums. An occasional gunshot was heard. The smells were captivating—mangoes, frying pork, banana leaves, and the ever-present fragrance of burning charcoal.

Though Haiti had just been through a hurricane and a coup, the people roamed the streets like tourists looking for fresh fun.

Jeff turned to Michelle. "Are you sure we can find out where Francis lives?"

Michelle nodded. "No problem. I got directions while you were drooling over the food over there."

"What if he's is in the middle of his voodoo thing

when we get there?" Jeff asked.

"We'll have to interrupt." Warren laughed nervously. "His child is more important."

"I hope so," Jeff said. "I hope so."

❖❖❖❖❖❖❖

Walking rapidly up the mountain road, the nerve-racking sound of drums pounded louder and louder. Jeff turned around and saw the harbor below.

Higher still, they walked past banks of flaming bougainvilleas and a rich tangle of vines and ravines. Making the final turn, they saw peasants smoking pipes and selling flowers. Then they headed down a very narrow road.

As they neared the priest's home, Jeff realized they were walking into Satan's territory.

The road wove around some old houses, then into an open area. Jeff stopped in his tracks. Right before him was another voodoo temple like the one they'd seen earlier. About 25 people were gathered in some ceremony.

Looking closer, he saw Francis holding a squirming goat in his hands. Michelle gasped. "I don't think you'll like this part."

Jeff turned his head quickly, as did Warren. But Jeff was too curious. Glancing up, he saw the goat's head hanging to one side. It fell limply to the ground. The drums became deafening.

Jeff froze in his tracks. "What should we do?" he cried. "Do you think he knows about Max?"

"I don't think so," Michelle replied. "He holds

ceremonies every night. If she'd been at her grand-mother's, he wouldn't know she was missing."

"We can't interrupt his ceremony," Jeff said.

"You're right," Warren agreed. He turned to Michelle. "How long do these meetings usually last?"

"Sometimes all night," she said. "We can wait a while. Since there aren't many people here, it should be short."

"I've got an idea." Jeff snapped his fingers. "Let's have our own meeting. We can break the power of the ceremony while we wait."

Warren and Michelle looked at each other. They shrugged their shoulders, then joined hands.

Time passed slowly, but soon Jeff felt a strange peace. He turned to Warren. "It's been about thirty minutes," he said. "And..."

Suddenly, the drums stopped. Everything became strangely quiet. The only drums they heard were in the distance, probably at other temples around the city.

Jeff stared at Michelle and Warren, then toward the temple. Everyone slowly left. Moments later, only Francis remained.

Suddenly, Jeff saw something amazing. A bright-ness hovered over the temple. "Look, you guys," he cried. "That light wasn't there when we came. Our prayers did that. God is here. The Bible says God inhabits the praises of His people."

Michelle smiled. "You're right, Jeff. Something was broken. I've never seen that before. It must be why the meeting ended so fast."

"What now?" Jeff asked.

"Let's go talk to him," Warren suggested.

As they walked toward the priest, Jeff noticed the angry look on his face.

"What do you want?" Frencis demanded. "Why are you here?"

Warren stepped in to face Francis. "Your daughter has had an accident."

"Couldn't be my daughter," Francis said, shaking his head. "Max is at her grandmother's. What do you mean, an accident?"

"She's been shot..."

"Shot!" Francis screamed. "What have you done? I knew you were trouble!"

"Calm down, sir. We had nothing to do with it."

"All right, all right. I'm calm. Are you sure it's Max? Just tell me what happened."

"Yes. I'm sure it's Max. She was on the docks a few hours ago, on an errand for her grandmother."

Francis set his jaw but didn't interrupt.

"She was hit by a stray bullet," Warren continued. "It hit her in the leg. She was bleeding heavily, so we took her to the ship. Doctors have already removed the bullet. She'll be fine."

"Why didn't you come earlier?" Francis demanded. "And what right do you have butting into my business?"

Jeff couldn't hold back any more. "Sir, Max could have bled to death. If we'd left her in the streets, she could have died."

The priest started throwing things in boxes. Suddenly, he whirled around. His eyes were squinty and dark. "I want her brought here immediately."

Jeff felt goosebumps pop up on his back.

"She just came out of anesthetic," Warren said. "The doctors need to watch her overnight. She needs rest."

The priest looked infuriated. "I'll come down to see for myself," he said quickly. Then he hesitated. "Never mind. I don't want anything to do with you or that ship of yours. You just have her back here first thing in the morning, or...."

Jeff looked at Warren in concern, hoping Francis wouldn't finish his sentence.

"And one more thing," the priest muttered.

Jeff looked into his glazed eyes, waiting.

The priest moved close. Too close for Jeff. "Don't even try to influence my daughter with your American religion."

Jeff felt sudden fear. He knew the others did too.

Warren moved closer. "Our medical team will deliver her as soon as she's well enough to travel."

"I said in the morning, didn't I? Now get out of here!" he said, throwing his hands in the air. He stomped off.

Jeff let out a sigh of relief. He was glad that was over. At least for now.

❖❖❖❖❖❖❖

The breakfast bell rang loudly. Jeff yawned, knowing he had slept right through the alarm. Wiping sleep from his eyes, he figured it was Saturday morning. They had been on the ship for a week.

He gazed out the porthole. It was beautiful outside, but the heat was already blazing. Jeff noticed

K.J. rolling around in the bunk below him and laughed.

"Sleepy head," he said. "We're going to miss breakfast if we don't hurry. I ask you. What's more important? Food or sleep?"

K.J. turned over. Then Jeff tossed a pillow at him. K.J. rolled over again, moaning louder.

"Hey. Get off my case," K.J. protested. "I'm really tired."

Jeff snickered and jumped out of bed.

❖❖❖❖❖❖❖

After breakfast, Dan stood up and asked for prayer requests and reports.

Jeff loved listening to all the staff's stories of the previous days' activities. Food had been off-loaded, and distribution of toys and supplies had begun. Clinics had been set up in three villages. Wounds were being treated and houses rebuilt. Jeff was amazed at what could be accomplished when people worked together.

Standing to his feet, Jeff couldn't wait another moment. "Please pray for the young girl who was shot yesterday. Her name is Max, er, Maxine. She's going to be fine. But her dad, Francis, is one of the most powerful voodoo priests in Haiti."

A murmur went through the group. As Jeff continued the story, no one moved until he was finished. The meeting was brought to completion after a prayer time. As soon as they were dismissed, the club hurried to the ward to see Maxine.

As they walked in, the girl flashed a wide smile.

Jeff wanted to tell Maxine about Jesus, but he remembered her father's stern warning. Bending over, he shook her hand. Smiling, Mindy sat on the edge of the bed and held the other one. K.J. stood at her side.

"My name is Jeff Caldwell. We found you bleeding on the street. The doctor said you'll be fine. How do you feel?"

After Michelle interpreted Jeff's words, Max spoke some words in Creole.

"She's feeling better," Michelle translated. "And she wants to thank you for helping her."

Jeff smiled. "Tell her we spoke to her father last night. We'll be taking her home today."

Michelle did so. "She says she had a great time with Mindy and K.J. last night after she woke up," Michelle told the group. "She understands some English and understood what they told her about God."

Jeff gasped, turning a little pale.

He looked at K.J. and Mindy, who had tears in her eyes.

Jeff was happy they had told Maxine about the Lord. But he knew there would be trouble now.

Max went on in Creole. Michelle laughed, after listening to her. "She likes being on the ship and would love to go on a voyage someday."

Everyone laughed.

Mindy pointed to Maxine's leg, which was wrapped in a clean, white cast. "How does it feel?"

Max grinned. "It feeels gooood," she said, patting the bumpy hardness of her cast.

Everyone smiled at her attempt to speak English.

Suddenly, Warren ran in with a very troubled look.

"What's wrong?" Jeff asked.

"Major Bennett is coming to the ship at noon."

"Why?" Mindy asked.

"He thinks we're all part of the CIA!"

Chapter 12

Inspection

Jeff leaned against the wall, stunned.

"Us?" Mindy scoffed. "Do we look connected to the Central Intelligence Agency? I'd think the CIA has enough brains to not use a bunch of kids."

"Well," Jeff took a deep breath, "they gather secret information for the U.S government. Major Bennett must think we know some secret."

"Seems logical to me," K.J. said, laughing. "The CIA doesn't have a very good reputation around the world. They might just need our help."

"This is serious, K.J.!" Mindy glared at him. "Why would Major Bennett think that? We're volunteers."

Max mumbled a few words to Michelle.

"Max wants to know what happened."

Jeff glanced back at her. "Tell her not to worry."

Jeff wished he could believe his own words. Why was everything going wrong again? He couldn't shake a nagging suspicion that Dr. Simpson was somehow responsible for this. But he would have to wait and see.

All morning, the ship was buzzing with activity. By eleven o'clock, the doctors at the hospital had already performed six surgeries. The team had said their goodbyes to Max. Warren and one of the nurses had taken her home in a tap tap.

Jeff, Mindy, K.J., and Michelle strolled along on the Promenade deck while they waited for the noon briefing.

"Michelle," Jeff said, "has the CIA been involved here before?"

Michelle laughed. "Probably. But most nations don't want anything to do Haiti."

"What do you mean?"

"When the Communists came to the Caribbean, Russia and Cuba didn't even mess with Haiti because of our leaders."

"Tell us more," Mindy said. "I always want to hear stories like this."

Michelle smiled shyly. "We studied in school about Papa Doc. I remember he came into power on September 27, 1957."

"Papa Doc?" K.J. laughed. "What a strange name for a leader."

"Francois Duvalier. He was a country doctor who came to power and ruled with an iron hand. He always had physical problems like weak eyes, heart problems, and diabetes. Though he began okay, he shed more blood than any leader we've had. It seems to be our history."

"Keep going," Mindy urged.

"Papa Doc was a black man who started as an honest voice for the poor. But then he gathered a group of thugs called Tonton's Macounte. They killed, tortured, and wiped out anyone that stood in his way.

"Really?" Mindy gasped.

"Papa Doc always dressed in black funeral clothes. He thought he was the god of death, and he even rewrote the Lord's prayer—making himself the Lord."

"Did your family suffer?" K.J. asked.

"No. But he had one family killed simply because they had the same last name as one of his enemies."

"What happened to Papa Doc?" Jeff wanted to know.

"He died. Then his son Jean-Claude came to power. He was called Baby Doc. He wasn't any better. He and his wife, whose name was Michelle...I always hated that part...stole millions of dollars. They hid it in Swiss bank accounts. Finally, he fled to France in 1987."

"Wow," K.J. said. "These guys were terrible."

Michelle nodded. "They called them both 'Presidents for Life.' But that didn't last long. After Baby Doc fled, the people tore open Papa Doc's tomb and stole the body."

"Well." Mindy laughed. "Evil men don't last long."

"My country's had a stream of bad leaders." Michelle rested her chin in her hands. "That's why we've had so many coups."

Jeff thought momentarily, absorbing the new information. "I think it all has to do with that ceremony to dedicate the country to Satan in 1791. The leaders need to break that thing and turn from voodoo. It's caused bloodshed and death here for too long."

"You're right, Jeff," Michelle said. "You're so right."

Jeff looked at the time. "It's almost noon. Time for the meeting. We have to make those military guys understand this is just an innocent Christian ship."

As Jeff started up the steps to the meeting area, he was nearly knocked over by Dr. Simpson, who came bounding down them two at a time. One of his bags smacked Jeff in the shoulder.

Something strange was going on, but Jeff couldn't figure it out.

Captain Davidson and Dan appeared with Major Bennett and three men in brown uniforms. They walked to the front of the meeting room.

Dan took his place at the podium. "Major Bennett is here on serious business. He's asked to speak to us."

Holding his hat, Major Bennett marched forward. "I'm sorry about the inspection. I don't believe it myself, but we've had another report about possible spies on your ship."

Everyone was shocked. Whispers filled the room.

"I'm grateful for your work with my people so far," Major Bennett continued. "But I'm under strict orders. We will be checking passports and searching rooms again."

He looked down at his shiny brown boots. "Your leaders have been very helpful. I'm sorry to take you away from your work, but you'll have to wait here until we've finished the inspection."

About two o'clock, Dan rushed back into the lounge where the crew was singing songs. He walked up to Jeff. "Have you seen Dr. Simpson?"

"Just before the meeting, I saw him racing down the stairs. Why?"

"His room is cleaned out. No one knows where he's gone."

Jeff stared at Dan in disbelief. "I just know Dr. Simpson is involved in all of this."

Dan nodded glumly, looking very unsettled.

Chapter 13

Mercy in Action

That afternoon, Jeff and the club videotaped people arriving for interviews, check-ups, and medical care. While the cameras were rolling, Major Bennett spotted Michelle and approached.

"I hope you're having a good day," the major said.

Michelle grinned charmingly. They were chatting when Marie's mother carried Marie up the ramp. Behind her blanket, part of her little face was exposed.

Major Bennett stopped.

Michelle noticed his discomfort. "Would you like to meet Marie?"

The mother looked embarrassed, but Michelle took Marie and proudly pulled the blanket away from her face. "You won't know her in a few days."

"Why's that?" the major asked.

"She's having an operation. Her lip will be normal."

Major Bennett stared in wonder. "I didn't know you did work like this!"

Michelle's eyes sparkled at him. "We specialize in cleft lip and palate operations."

Major Bennett stumbled for words. This hard man looked as if he might cry. He spoke to Michelle in Creole for a minute, then he and Michelle walked off by themselves.

Jeff was exploding inside. He was used to being the first one to know what was going on. The longer they were gone, the more his curiosity grew.

After a half hour, Michelle and Major Bennett returned. He said a quick goodbye, then left with his men.

Michelle's eyes sparkled and the glow on her face looked as if it might catch fire.

"What was that all about?" Jeff immediately asked.

"Major Bennett was touched deeply by Marie. He told me his story."

"What story?" Mindy said. "Details, girl. Details!"

Michelle plopped into a chair and everyone encircled her. "Major Bennett has a ten-year-old son. He was born with a severe cleft palate. It causes sinus and eating problems that create stress for the whole family. The major never had enough money for an operation, and he's ashamed. He thought his boy would have to spend the rest of his life like that."

"Yeah," K.J. said. "Go on."

"Well," Michelle grinned, "I showed him the pictures of the children in the ward."

Everyone waited.

"He asked us to operate on his son. Of course, the doctors were delighted to help. He's bringing him onboard to be examined."

Jeff's heart danced. God was at work.

Later, Jeff and the others piled into the back of a truck loaded with food. K.J. immediately pointed his camera out the back. They were accompanying a relief team from the ship into a poor village.

Jeff couldn't wait to hand out the food and supplies. He loved watching God's love in action. As they bounced along the rutted path, he was glad to be alive—and glad Michelle was along to help them understand Haiti.

Jeff glanced at her. "Did Haiti look like this when you lived here?"

Michelle frowned. "No. It's getting worse."

"What do you mean?" Jeff asked.

"I remember lots more beautiful coffee trees. They've been used for firewood. The slopes that were so fertile are now barren hills because of the erosion. The people are self-destructing."

As the village neared, Jeff noticed the shabby shacks they'd seen along the way were piles of rubble here. When the truck came to a stop, the staff jumped down and set up tables to feed the people. Instantly, a crowd gathered.

K.J. and Michelle went to work setting up the equipment, preparing to tape the food distribution.

Suddenly, Jeff saw something move in the shadows. It was a pair of skinny brown shoulders appearing from the dark corner of a building.

The boy looked about 12 years old, and he was naked. He stumbled, zigzagging toward the truck. The lower half of his body was powdered with gray dust. His hair was reddish and matted. The flesh on his torso was almost translucent—a thin, inadequate cover for his rib cage.

Jeff had to turn away. The boy stopped, then looked up at Jeff. He made a mangled sound. His leg bounced under him, and he hit at his knee to make it stop. His eyes were flat and gray. Putting his hand up to his hair, he yanked at it.

Jeff couldn't move. He yelled for Michelle. Moving closer to the boy, Jeff looked into his eyes.

"Ask him his name," he said to Michelle.

A mumbling groan came from the boy. Michelle asked again.

She looked at Jeff and turned her head to wipe away a tear. "I think it's Joseph."

Jeff's heart ached. "We've got to do something. Food won't be enough. He's going to die if he stays here."

Michelle focused on Jeff again. "There are lots of kids like this in Haiti. Most of them die very young."

"We've got to bring him back to the ship," Jeff insisted. "The doctors will help him. He needs food and rest."

They helped Joseph to the back of the truck, found him a place to lie down, then brought him a plate of chicken, rice, and beans.

Throughout the day, Jeff saw people who were nearly as ill as Joseph. On camera, he and Michelle interviewed people about what the hurricane had done to their homes and families. Mindy took notes as fast as her fingers could type on her laptop.

By 4:30 in the afternoon, K.J. was nearly out of film and the truck was nearly empty. But the lines of people were still very long.

"This is so sad," Michelle said. "There is no end to the need here. The teams will have to come back tomorrow. We have to go."

❖❖❖❖❖❖❖

When they returned to the ship, Jeff ran to get a stretcher for Joseph. After examining the boy, the medical staff decided to admit him to the ward.

"What about his parents?" Jeff asked. "Shouldn't we contact them?"

Michelle shook her head sadly. "His parents left him a long time ago."

Jeff felt deep grief. The group sat with Joseph a while in silence.

"I don't know about you," Jeff finally said, "but I'm beat.

"Me too," Mindy agreed.

"But I'm happy on the inside," Michelle said. "I think we made some difference out there today."

"That's for sure," Jeff replied. "A tired happiness."

❖❖❖❖❖❖❖

Early Sunday morning, Jeff felt new energy. Ten hours of sleep made him excited to get to work.

Warren met them in the dining room at breakfast. Because he'd been out late with another team, he hadn't seen them since early the day before.

"How'd it go yesterday?" Warren asked.

The team spent 30 minutes talking about Joseph and the feeding program. When Dan strode in, Jeff remembered the doctor.

"Has anyone found Dr. Simpson yet?" he asked.

Dan frowned. "Yeah. We just found out he hopped a plane."

"What happened to him?" Jeff prodded.

"He left the country."

Chapter 14

Betrayal

Jeff gasped in amazement. "How could he do that? I thought the purser had his passport."

Dan lowered his head. "Yeah. That's the way it's supposed to work. But he told her he needed to check something on it and just never gave it back to her."

"That guy was strange," Mindy said. "Do you have people like him very often?"

"Not often." Dan smiled. "But people are still people. Our staff have five months of solid training. After all that, we know them well. But when some kind of disaster hits, we need outside help. It's hard to check everyone out completely."

"Yeah," K.J. said, glancing at Mindy. "They let you on."

Mindy smiled sweetly, then leaned over and punched K.J. in the arm. "You shouldn't talk, K.J.! You've nearly gotten us kicked out of several countries, as I recall."

Everyone laughed.

"Hey, did you hear about Major Bennett's son?" Jeff asked Dan. "Will the doctors operate soon?"

"Yes, I heard." Dan glanced at his watch. "Today's Sunday. The major is bringing his boy in tomorrow."

"Tomorrow!" Mindy yelped. "That's quick!"

"No." Dan grinned. "Paperwork first. And a physical. If all goes well, he'll have surgery Wednesday."

"That's exciting," Mindy said, bouncing up and down. "And we'll be here. I can't wait."

Dan turned to Warren. "You and the club will be here until Saturday, right?"

Warren nodded. "That's the plan. But who knows what could happen?"

Everyone laughed nervously.

"I'll be sad to leave," Mindy declared. "I'd love to stay for the next three months. I could live on this ship forever."

"Now there's a thought." K.J. smiled.

Mindy smacked K.J. again.

"Ouch," K.J. groaned. "Sorry. I was only kidding."

Dan checked his watch again. "It's nearly nine hundred hours. That little Haitian church starts in just over an hour. You guys had better get going if you're going to ride with our music team."

Everyone left to get ready.

❖❖❖❖❖❖❖

On the way over to the Haitian church, Jeff smoothed the wrinkles out of his grey slacks and striped shirt. He wondered how a church could survive with all the voodoo around.

When they arrived, they were warmly greeted by the pastor, a small Haitian man dressed in an old suit. K.J. and Mindy helped the music team set up their equipment, then they gathered for prayer. Michelle and Jeff discussed what to say. Jeff decided to talk on prayer.

As the meeting began, Jeff felt the powerful presence of the Lord. After the ship's band led the worship music, the pastor introduced Jeff and Michelle, who would be translating.

As they walked up together, Jeff gave Michelle's hand a gentle squeeze. Even though they had only met two weeks earlier, he really appreciated her.

Jeff quickly scanned the crowd. A lot of women sat in the rows, many holding more than one child. Jeff didn't see many men.

"I'm glad to be here," Jeff began. "I'm not as talented as the musicians, but I am a part of a club called Reel Kids."

He introduced the club members. K.J. said a few words, then went back to his familiar place behind the camera. Mindy told the crowd about Marie, the baby with the cleft palate. By the time Mindy finished, every mother in the place was in tears. The place got quiet as she sat down.

Jeff stood again, looking at the focused crowd. "As you know, we're from America. We've heard much about Haiti in the news. And we've seen so much since we've been here."

Michelle translated and Jeff went on. "God's power is greater than the power of voodoo. Because we have the Spirit of God, we don't fear any other spirits. I believe God wants to break the past curse on Haiti."

As Jeff waited for the translation, all eyes were on him. Michelle looked at Jeff, raising her brow.

"Jesus said He would build His church," he continued, "and the gates of hell would not prevail against it."

Jeff then described his dream, telling of the bright light that overcame the snake. Finally Jeff had everyone come to the front and join hands. Leading them in prayer to renounce the curse on the land, he proclaimed Jesus Lord over Haiti.

Michelle burst into tears. Mindy scrambled over to hold her, crying as well.

"Jeff, I discovered something as you were praying," Michelle confided in him. "Before we left L.A., I didn't want to come here because of what I experienced when I was little. But something warmed my heart. It felt like the light you talked about. Now I feel bright inside. I've got passion to pray for Haiti like never before."

As Jeff gave her a hug, tears came to his eyes.

Mindy handed out Kleenex. Michelle needed several.

"I felt the Lord spoke," Michelle finally said. "He wants me to be a voice for the needs of Haiti. He wants me to recruit a band of prayer warriors from all over the world."

Jeff watched more tears flow. Tears of joy.

❖❖❖❖❖❖❖

After breakfast on Monday morning, Jeff and K.J. made themselves comfortable on the deck to prepare the cameras for the day's shoot. They wanted to be ready when Major Bennett arrived with his son. Later, they planned to help a team who were setting up another village clinic.

Jeff was so grateful to be alive—*really* alive. He was happy and fulfilled. He knew his life had a purpose. He thought of some of his friends back home whose biggest goal in life seemed to be getting up in the morning. Not him. Never a dull or spare moment.

Jeff's thoughts were interrupted when he saw Francis, the voodoo priest, hurrying up the gangway. Two angry-looking Haitian men followed at his heels.

Jeff glanced around, but none of the other club members had noticed yet.

Francis strutted up to Jeff. When he stopped with his hands on his hips, Mindy realized he was there. So did Michelle.

K.J. had been shining the camcorder. While looking the priest in the eye, K.J. flicked the button to turn it on, pointing it right at Francis.

Francis began an angry tirade. "You guys were spotted praying near my temple!"

Jeff didn't say a word.

"And someone told me what you said about voodoo in church yesterday," Francis went on.

A whisper of fear came over Jeff.

Francis's eyes flickered. "Maybe you helped my daughter, but interfering in Haitian ways can be dangerous."

The other men stared daggers through Jeff.

Mindy and Michelle listened in silence. Jeff hoped they were praying.

Francis bent over to get eye to eye with Jeff. "The spirits are not happy. These two priests have agreed to join me in asking the spirits to bring harm on all of you unless you leave now."

As suddenly as they had come, Francis and the two others turned and started down the gangway. K.J. rotated the camera an inch to the left to catch their exit, then flicked it off.

Jeff slumped into his deck chair. He felt numb. Frightened.

"Did you hear that?" Mindy finally cried.

"Satan is mad," Michelle said. "Really mad."

"Yeah," Jeff agreed. "But we're not goin' down. Let's go talk to Dan and Warren."

Just then, Jeff saw Captain Davidson, Warren, and Dan get out of a tap tap and start for the ship. Frantically, Jeff waved at them. The team ran to meet them on the dock.

Jeff looked for the angry priests, but they had vanished into the crowd.

Suddenly, military vehicles roared up, screeching their tires, followed by a van loaded with soldiers. Inside, Major Bennett sat with another man whose uniform was decorated with lots of ribbons and medals.

Jeff was excited to see the major, but he wondered where his wife and son were.

Dan turned back to meet them. Jeff was confused when he saw the tense look on Major Bennett's face. Gone were the cordial smile and friendly attitude.

Major Bennett marched toward Captain Davidson. Warren walked over to Jeff.

"This is General Duval," Major Bennett said, turning toward the stiff Haitian officer. "He's my commanding officer."

Jeff stepped back.

"General Duval has just received proof of government spies on your ship," Major Bennett went on. "We've identified one already. A Dr. Simpson. We suspect there are more."

Jeff almost jumped out of his skin.

Major Bennett's face tightened as he looked from face to face. He shook his head sadly. "I thought you were for real. But that's over now. I have orders concerning you."

"What's that, sir?" Dan asked.

Jeff leaned in.

"You're under arrest," Major Bennett smirked.

Chapter 15

Darkness

The color drained from Dan's face. Captain Davidson took a small step back.

Dan dropped his head for a second, then looked into the major's eyes. "Sir, there's been a mistake. We had no idea Dr. Simpson was a spy."

The look Jeff saw on Major Bennett's face said he didn't believe it. "We'll find out, won't we?"

"What about your son?" Dan asked calmly. "We want to go ahead with the operation."

Major Bennett laughed. "I'm sorry. I'd never trust you with my boy now."

No one knew what to say. Sadness and silence fell over the group.

"Everyone must stay onboard," Major Bennett commanded. "You will cease all activities on land. The team that lives here is also under house arrest."

After giving further orders, the major ducked into the van and left.

The soldiers pushed everyone up the gangplank, then spread out everywhere. Jeff knew they were in hot water now.

❖❖❖❖❖❖❖

In a state of shock, Jeff stared quietly out the window from the meeting lounge. Dark clouds hovered over Port-au-Prince.

Dan walked in and faced his confused crew. "We have to keep up our faith. Since Haiti is in turmoil, trouble is to be expected. We're trying to contact some U.S. officials, hoping they will intervene."

Murmurs flew through the anxious crowd. Sniffles came from one corner of the room.

Dan cleared his throat. "God's Word says to praise Him in all circumstances. So let's start praising the Lord. The best thing we can do is to turn the ship into a giant prayer meeting."

Jeff nodded in agreement. As he stared out the window, the sky looked darker yet—like it was night. He wondered if the darkness related to his dream.

Then an idea came to him. After thinking about it for a few moments, he decided he had to share it. He timidly raised his hand. Dan nodded to him and he stood.

"A few days ago," Jeff said, "I had a dream. God

showed me His desire to defeat the powers of darkness in Haiti."

Jeff went on, sharing the details of his dream. Everyone listened intently.

"For the last few days, I've wrestled to discover what the bright light means." Jeff's mind was going at a furious pace. "I finally understand. First, it stands for God's justice. The Haitian people were horribly mistreated in the past."

He cleared his throat and went on. "Africans were kidnapped and forced onto ships. Many died crossing the ocean. Those who lived were forced to work as slaves."

Out of the corner of his eye, Jeff watched Michelle. She had her head down.

"As members of the white race, I believe we need to ask God's forgiveness. Though we personally weren't alive then, we must identify with the white race. Sadly, many slave owners claimed to be Christians."

As he listened to the silence in the room, Jeff also heard weeping. "The light in my dream speaks of the power of prayer. It is the only thing that can change Haiti. Unless our hearts are free from past sin and prejudice, our prayers won't be heard."

Jeff glanced at Warren, who stood like a proud father, nodding his head in agreement. Jeff waited for Dan to say something. Everyone waited in silence. The weeping got louder.

Dan reached for the microphone. "I think Jeff is onto something. Our efforts to reach Haiti for Jesus can't work unless there is enough prayer cover. God's light will become brighter and brighter when we pray with clean hearts."

Some people nodded, others cried together.

"Michelle had an idea the other day," Jeff added. "God wants to send hundreds of prayer teams to Haiti until the land is free from the deal they made with the devil."

Jeff slowly sat down. Several others got up to read Scripture verses or share thoughts. They all focused on the idea of forgiveness.

Dan scanned the room one final time. "I think it's clear what the Lord wants us to do here. Let's go to prayer now."

Everyone bowed their heads. One by one, staff members began to stand to ask forgiveness for things they had said or done to each other. Others needed to be forgiven for feelings they held against each other.

Then they asked God to forgive all the sins of the white race. Jeff leaned over to Michelle, who was sobbing. As he took her hand, he got an idea. After sharing it with her, they walked forward.

Dan quietly handed Jeff the microphone. He took a deep breath and turned to Michelle.

"Michelle," Jeff said softly. "I'm here representing the white race. Since you represent the black race, I want to say how sorry I am for the way we treated you. Our behavior was shameful. We gave your people no choice but to trust in darkness to defeat slavery in Haiti."

Michelle was sobbing, and everyone cried with her. Then Michelle wiped away her tears and reached for the mike. She stood tall and squared her shoulders.

"I forgive you, Jeff," she said boldly. "And I ask

forgiveness for my people. We hated you..." Before she could finish, tears began again.

Jeff knew her heart said it all. He reached out and hugged her gently.

Finally, Michelle looked up. Her eyes were shining. "I want everyone to forgive me. I want my heart to be clean too."

People began coming forward. One at a time, they confessed sins of bitterness, anger, hatred, and pride. After an hour, things seemed to slow down and Dan took the microphone.

"I think God has cleaned our hearts," Dan said. "We're ready to pray and praise the Lord now. The Bible says 'The effectual fervent prayers of a righteous man avails much.'"

Everyone applauded. Some prayed quietly, other prayed out loud.

Suddenly, Jeff was struck with another idea. He didn't want it to seem like he was taking over the whole meeting, yet he felt God was telling him to share the idea with the whole group.

Swallowing his discomfort, Jeff walked back up to the front and told Dan about it. Dan nodded and turned to the crowd. "Jeff has an idea I believe is from God. I've asked him to share it with us."

"I believe we have the key to Haiti," Jeff said. "If we're allowed off the ship, we should find the place where the ceremony dedicating the island to Satan took place in 1791. We can speak out forgiveness there. I believe something will be released."

Everyone nodded excitedly. Dan divided everyone into groups of six. For the next hour, fervent prayers filled the room and rose all the way from the ship to heaven.

Later, Jeff saw someone hand Dan a note. As Dan read it, a concerned look crossed his face. Then he approached Michelle. After talking, Dan nodded to Captain Davidson. Then the three of them walked out of the lounge.

Jeff's curiosity almost exploded within him. No matter how hard he tried to concentrate, he couldn't get them out of his mind. He had to find out what was going on.

K.J. was still praying with one of the marine mechanics, but Jeff talked Warren and Mindy into coming with him. They headed down the stairs, hoping for the best. As they walked toward the gangway, he looked outside. It was now pitch black. How could this be? he wondered. It was still day-time.

Military jeeps and vans waited outside. Jeff saw Major Bennett and General Duval getting into the van. Soldiers with guns escorted Michelle into the back.

Jeff felt confused, but he hoped everything was okay. When he saw the look on Dan's face, though, he knew it wasn't.

"What happened?" he cried. "Why are they taking Michelle?"

Dan shook his head sadly. "I'm sorry. Everything is much worse."

"What do you mean?" Jeff tried to say calm.

"They've given us twelve hours to sail."

Warren and Mindy gasped in unison. Jeff's heart sank. He felt as dark on the inside as the sky was dark outside.

"What about Michelle?" he groaned.

Dan hung his head. Finally he answered. "They think her passport is phony."

"Why did they take her away?" Mindy wailed.

"She's been arrested."

Chapter 16

Revolution for Life

"What about our prayer time?" Jeff exploded. "Doesn't God care about that?"

Jeff stared at Dan. His eyes looked weary and pained, but he took a deep breath and headed back to inform the crew. The team followed in shocked, confused silence.

❖❖❖❖❖❖❖

"Our only choice," Dan said after explaining what had happened, "is to prepare to sail."

After hearing those words, Jeff stumbled slowly

to his cabin. Feeling hopeless, he flopped across his bunk. His heart felt darker than it looked outside.

He couldn't believe they were preparing to leave. Their mission had just begun, and now Satan was driving them out.

K.J. and Mindy knocked softly on the door. Mumbling, he told them to come in.

"I feel terrible," Jeff cried. "What about all that stuff I said in church Sunday? I don't know if even I believe it any more! I just don't understand what God is doing here."

"Haiti must be out of our league." Mindy raised her chin. "Maybe the situation is hopeless because Satan has been in control for two hundred years."

"That's not true, you guys." K.J. became angry. "God will come through somehow. He always does."

Jeff nodded reluctantly. "What does Warren want us to do?" he asked. "We were supposed to fly home, not sail with the ship anyway."

K.J. laughed, shaking his head. "Forget that. We only have one choice, and that's sail."

Mindy suddenly became angry. "I'm not leaving Michelle."

❖❖❖❖❖❖❖

It was ten at night. The ship was scheduled to sail in less than two hours. Time passed rapidly as the crew busily prepared for departure.

Suddenly, a voice boomed over the loudspeaker. "This is the captain speaking. Please meet in the lounge in five minutes for an emergency meeting."

Jeff groaned at the others. "What now?" he cried, getting up.

❖❖❖❖❖❖❖

Sitting in the lounge, Jeff bit his fingernails. Then Dan walked in. And he was smiling.

Jeff glanced at K.J. and Mindy hopefully. K.J. shot him an I-told-you-so look but didn't say a word.

Dan took the microphone. "God has made some dramatic changes on our behalf."

Jeff leaned forward. For the first time in hours, he smiled.

"Major Bennett was just here," Dan went on. "General Duval received a call an hour ago from the United States. The CIA has cleared up the confusion. Turns out that Dr. Simpson was once a CIA agent who had some kind of mixup in Haiti before. Seems they kicked him off the force years ago. I have no idea what for."

Jeff's mouth hung open.

"Missions International and—get this—" Dan paused dramatically, "the United States of America have both issued an apology for this embarrassment. They'll be sending additional funds to aid the hurricane victims."

A whoop went up around the room.

Dan calmed the crowd, then continued. "Major Bennett says we can stay as long as we want."

Jeff's hand shot into the air. "What about Michelle?"

Dan grinned widely. "After checking out her passport, they've released her too. She should be back here in a few minutes."

The crowd cheered and praised the Lord.

❖❖❖❖❖❖❖

Several days later, bright sunshine lit up the skies. Jeff and Mindy raced to meet K.J. and his camera in the hospital ward. When they screeched to a halt, Jeff saw the beaming smile on Michelle's face.

In her arms, she cuddled little Marie. The bandages had been removed from her face. A tiny red scar marked the spot where her deformed lip had been. Her face was almost perfect. As if on cue, Marie smiled and cooed for the team.

In the next room, Joseph was sitting up in his bed. After only a few days onboard the ship, he hardly looked like the malnourished boy they had brought in from the village.

Major Bennett's son, Jean, was there too. Though still bandaged, his operation had gone perfectly. Jeff knew that behind those bandages, there was a big smile.

Max was there for a checkup, sitting beside Jean. K.J. put down his camera long enough to sign her cast. Her leg healing fast, but even more importantly, Jeff knew Max had seen the light—the bright light of Jesus.

In the last few days, Haitians had stopped coming to her dad's temple because they felt bad spirits there. Now, even Francis was questioning the power of voodoo. It was a miracle.

K.J. got a shot of Dan and Warren standing together with their arms folded across their chests. They looked like new fathers about to pass out cigars.

Suddenly, Jeff jumped up excitedly. "I've got an idea! Well, it's partly what Michelle suggested."

"What's that?" Dan cocked his head to the side.

"Since Major Bennett has invited us back again soon, let's have an outreach. We could invite hundreds of kids from around the world. Let's call it 'Haiti for Jesus!'"

Everyone nodded while Jeff rattled on. "We'll surround Haiti with prayer teams. It will be changed forever."

Warren gleamed in approval. Michelle beamed.

"It'll be a new revolution! This one will be a revolution for life! Eternal life!" Jeff's eyes flickered with joy.

"Yeah," Michelle added. "Haitians should know Jesus is the real President for Life."

Everyone nodded. Jeff knew he'd return soon.

And he knew he'd never forget Haiti.

Other
Reel Kids Adventures
by Dave Gustaveson

The Missing Video
An exciting adventure into Communist Cuba. Will the dark-eyed stranger send the "Reel Kids" into an international nightmare?

Mystery at Smokey Mountain
A spine-tingling mystery with the "Reel Kids" in the Philippines. Jeff and the "Reel Kids" become the target of wicked men as they attempt to help the poor at Smokey Mountain in Manila.

The Stolen Necklace
A stolen necklace, wild animals and a life-threatening African mystery will keep "Reel Kids" readers turning pages.

The Mysterious Case
Jeff Caldwell couldn't imagine how one small mistake would cost them. A mysterious suitcase leads them on a collision course with the dangerous Colombian drug cartel. Would the drug lords allow them to continue their mission?

The Amazon Stranger
The "Reel Kids" trip to South America had become far riskier than anyone could imagine. Would they escape the perils of the deadly river to reach the Amazon tribe?

OTHER RESOURCES:

You Can Change the World — $14.99
Colorful illustrations, facts, and stories help you understand and pray for people in other cultures and countries.

Tracking Your Walk — $9.99
This journal will help you record your prayers and thoughts and encourage you to pray for people around the world. Includes maps and country information.

For information to help you go on your own adventure:
Kings Kids
P.O. Box 8000-569
Sumas, WA 98295

For Youth With A Mission's outreach opportunities, send for the *GO MANUAL*.
Send $4.00 to:
YWAM Publishing
P.O. Box 55787
Seattle, WA 98155

For information on Youth With A Mission's ship ministry:
Mercy Ships
P.O. Box 2020
Lindale, TX 75771-2020
Phone: 1 (800) 772-SHIP